"LET ME DOWN, YOU JERKS!"

The four taflak, natives of the planet Majesty, who were carrying Berdan obliged him. They dropped the squirming boy into a huge fire-hardened clay cauldron of cold water, around the soot-stained base of which small twigs, dried leaves, and many larger branches had been piled. While several of the creatures held him in the pot, others began to light a fire underneath it. A medium-sized taflak, passing a broad platter from tentacle to tentacle, dumped it into the pot. Berdan shivered as he stared down at the chopped-up berries and shoots bobbing in the water all around him.

Somehow, he had the feeling he wasn't about to take a bath . . .

BRIGHTSUIT MACBEAR

L. NEIL SMITH

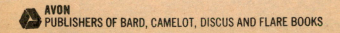
AVON
PUBLISHERS OF BARD, CAMELOT, DISCUS AND FLARE BOOKS

THIS BOOK IS FOR
Margaret L. Hamilton, the Wicked Witch of the North

CONTENTS

CHAPTER I: Mr. Meep 1
CHAPTER II: *Tom Edison Maru* 7
CHAPTER III: The Dead Past 16
CHAPTER IV: Happy Birthday, Berdan 27
CHAPTER V: Spoonbender's Museum 36
CHAPTER VI: Hot Pursuit 47
CHAPTER VII: The Sea of Leaves 55
CHAPTER VIII: Pemot 65
CHAPTER IX: Marooned 73
CHAPTER X: One Lam's Family 84
CHAPTER XI: The Gossamer Bomber 93
CHAPTER XII: Middle C 103
CHAPTER XIII: The Crankapillar 113
CHAPTER XIV: j'Kaimreks and the Baldies 123
CHAPTER XV: The Revolt of the Feebs 131
CHAPTER XVI: The Screwmaran 139
CHAPTER XVII: The Captain-Mother 148
CHAPTER XVIII: Is It Safe? 157
CHAPTER XIX: An Illuminating Experience 166
CHAPTER XX: Tunnel Rats 174
CHAPTER XXI: Well-Chosen Words 185
CHAPTER XXII: The Confederate Air Force 196
CHAPTER XXIII: Ruby Slippers 206

CHAPTER 1:
Mr. Meep

"I don't understand," the boy protested, "why can't we just spray-paint this chocolate sundae?"

After a morning's practice at the soda fountain, fifteen-year-old Berdan Geanar was sticky to the elbows with four dozen assorted flavors of ice cream and countless gooey toppings. His fingers were cold, cramped around the old-fashioned scoop. Before him on the stainless countertop were the remains of half a hundred failed "experiments."

By now, he almost looked forward to busing tables again after the lunch hour.

"Splay-paint sundae alla same!" His employer growled, peering with critical misgivings at Berdan's latest effort. Hours had dragged by under the restaurant owner's supervision. Berdan hadn't yet figured out what accent the old chimpanzee had chosen this morning.

"Mistah Meep food make by hand! Not make sundae all alike!"

The process which they both called spray-painting was the most common manufacturing method in the far-flung Galactic Confederacy. Berdan's well-worn smartsuit, cut down from adult size, adjusted at the moment to resemble the faded blue denim pattern the boy preferred and streaked below his apron with marshmallow and butterscotch, had been created by this process, along with the few other material pos-

awaiting a fresh shipment before evening. The squid served as the dolphin's "hands": Berdan could see circuit boxes, each no bigger than a coin and tuned to the mammal's voice, attached to the mantles of the molluscs.

Of all the intelligent species Berdan knew about, those discovered so far—or who'd discovered the Confederacy themselves—in the explored portion of the galaxy, the only ones not represented in Mr. Meep's huge kitchen at the moment were killer whales and lamviin. One *orca* worked on the night shift, the boy knew. The lamviin, most recent of the sentient races to be discovered, were still too few among the frontier planets and giant starships of the Confederacy to be seen often. If half of what he'd heard about their quick intelligence and enthusiasm for space exploration were true, that would be changing soon.

But what mattered—to Mr. Meep, to Berdan, to each occupant of the huge kitchen, and to the paying customers out front—was that everybody here had a unique talent, was good at something different. When someone like Mr. Meep, whose unique talent involved business organization, sorted it all out and put it back together again, as he'd been doing for at least a hundred years, the result was profitable to all participants—and unforgettable to the customers.

This morning Mr. Meep was sorting, and Berdan Geanar, the unfortunate sortee, was resigning himself to the fact that, whatever his unique—but so far undiscovered—talent turned out to consist of, he wasn't going to be a dessert chef. Just as well, the boy thought. His stomach felt queasy and he was sure his face was green. He didn't think he could ever look a scoop of strawberry jujube ice cream square in the maraschino cherry ever again as long as he lived.

Nevertheless, he wouldn't give up without a struggle. "But couldn't we *program* every sundae to be diff—"

"Ha!" Mr. Meep sneered. Folding his arms in front of his chest, he tucked his hands into opposing

cient sounding and impersonal, filled the boy's mind as if the woman had been standing right behind him.

"Berdan Geanar. Berdan Geanar. You're wanted at home. Berdan Geanar. Berdan Geanar. You're wanted at home. Berdan Geanar. Berdan Geanar. You're wanted—"

No one else had heard it.

They weren't intended to.

Berdan blinked, thinking thoughts which were, for him, the equivalent of picking up a telephone. "Message received."

He thought the words into the near-microscopic electronic implant which had been placed on the surface of his brain before he had been old enough to walk.

The implant, as powerful a computer as the one Mr. Meep wore on his wrist, relayed his reply to the dispatching service.

"Thank you—I think."

For a few moments, standing silent, the ice cream scoop still in his hand, he tried, with his mind, to reach his home number. He didn't get an answer and knew what that meant. It made him angry. He had work he'd promised to do, tables to wait—another personal service the Meep Family Restaurants were famous for—and, despite his embarrassing failure with desserts and the risk of tasting alien food, he liked this job. He needed it and didn't want to lose it.

As the individual who'd summoned him knew perfectly well.

With great reluctance, he rinsed his hands off in the stainless sink, thrust them through the drying membrane hanging over it, and shrugged out of his apron.

He turned to his employer. "I've gotta go home now, Mr. Meep. I'm real sorry. My grandfather's calling me."

Mr. Meep, who knew a good deal more about Berdan's personal problems than the boy realized, nod-

CHAPTER II:
Tom Edison Maru

The world was two miles tall and seven—not quite eight—miles in diameter for young Berdan Geanar, growing up aboard one of the giant starships of the expanding Galactic Confederacy.

Those were the dimensions of the *Tom Edison Maru*, the only world he'd ever known, a gleaming, dome-topped vessel of which Berdan himself, his employer Mr. Meep, and everyone else the boy had ever met, were "residents" or "crew," depending on who was describing the many humans, porpoises, killer whales, chimpanzees, orangutans, and gorillas aboard—not to mention the numerous alien species which those wandering Earth-born races had made their friends.

Inside, just like one of the layer cakes baked in the Meep Family ovens, the ship was divided into level upon level, some no taller, floor to ceiling, than the kitchen he'd just left, others so high vaulted that clouds sometimes formed within them. Rain—even snow on occasion—fell at times like that, over indoor forests and parklands planted by the ship's builders. Birds flew through the brilliant artificial skies, startled by weekend kite fliers or the odd passing hang glider.

If Berdan had thought to look up just now—his eyes, in fact, were on his feet—he might have seen a

to its politics and economics, had, at one time or another, been declared "impossible" by some expert.

Other channels buzzed with an unusual scandal, a break-in and theft at a scientific museum. Crime was rare in the fleet: instead of being imprisoned where they could learn from professionals, criminal beginners were expected to work, to pay—in a literal sense—for what they'd done. They never came to think of themselves as crooks but as people who'd made a mistake and made up for it. The widespread custom of carrying personal weapons discouraged crime, as well. Thus the media, enjoying a unique opportunity, were playing it for all it was worth.

Berdan, however, had other things to worry about. Compared with other times and places he might have been born, all the misery the human race had seen and suffered during its long, bloody history, it was a wonderful world he lived in. For the moment, however, the boy was blind to the wonder all about him, oblivious, in fact, to just about everything. His thoughts centered on how terrible he felt.

Mr. Meep's back entrance let out into a quiet, somewhat twisted corridor behind the restaurant. On this residential level, few of the streets—most fabricated from a springy synthetic substance, easy on the feet and decorated in bright colors—had been constructed in straight lines. They meandered about, wandering past homes and shops and other restaurants (none, in Berdan's opinion, as good as Mr. Meep's), following leisurely, scenic routes, with the idea of making the journey, whether by foot, by bicycle (a gorilla on a unicycle passed Berdan as he shambled along), or by small car, as important as the destination. Quicker means of transportation existed for those beings in a hurry.

Just as numerous, and meandering, were the many canals provided for the finny folk of the Confederacy. Here and there the color-paved pathways dipped, so people who followed along them could see into the water through thick transparencies set into decorative walls, and so the porpoises and killer whales

"Chickensquat!"

Berdan's unhappy ruminations were interrupted by a rude word he'd heard many times before. He looked up from the yellow, rubbery sidewalk on which he'd kept his eyes as he made his way home, and was surprised. His absentminded footsteps had brought him further than he'd intended, past three transport patches, almost home the hard way, to the center of Deejay Thorens Park. Far across its cultivated lawns, a brass band played from a whitewashed gazebo.

Unlike the people of many previous civilizations, the beings of the Confederacy tended to honor scientists, inventors, and philosophers, rather than soldiers or politicians, erecting statues, naming parks and streets and starships after them, preferring to single out those who were still alive to enjoy the tribute. Some exceptions disproved the rule: two levels above this, another park had been given the same name the starship itself bore, Thomas Alva Edison.

But this was Thorens Park, and, sure enough, right at the feet of its central feature, a life-sized statue of the galaxy's greatest (and most beautiful) physicist, the woman who'd discovered the principle which drove this vessel between the stars, sat its other central feature, a rumpled study in gray and black, just as he always seemed to be, on a violet-colored park bench.

Old Captain Forsyth. Rumors which had almost grown into legends claimed the old fellow had once been a fearsome warrior of great accomplishment. Now he was in his usual place, silent and immovable as the statue itself, reading an old-fashioned hardcopy newspaper. Even from where he stood, Berdan could read headlines about the museum theft and the new planet, Majesty. He'd often wondered whether the ancient chimpanzee ever went home, or whether he even had a home.

"Slimy loops of DNA!

"Spell 'em out—whaddo they say?

"What's in genes won't go away!

seemed, for some strange reason of his own, to accept it.

The pair either side of Geeky shook with theatrical laughter and began chanting *"Chickensquat! Chickensquat!"* in a way which kept Berdan from answering, just as they intended, even if he'd thought of something clever to say. He gave up, shrugged, and stepped forward, intending to pass between them and be on his way.

"Hey, Chickensquat!" Someone grabbed Berdan by the arm.

The complaint—and the grab—came from Kenjon "Crazy" Zovich, in some ways the worst of the three. He was nicknamed (although no one Berdan knew had ever dared say it to his face) not just for his nasty sense of humor, but because he possessed a violent, unpredictable temper (or it possessed him) when other people didn't think his jokes were funny or tried to play jokes on him.

"Hey, Chickensquat, you oughta know by now," Zovich warned him, holding on to Berdan's arm, "we ain't gonna let you off that easy, Chicken-chicken-squat-squat!"

He danced in place around Berdan, turning him as he went.

"We ain't even *close* to through with you!"

Berdan seized the offending hand by the fingertips and peeled it off his arm, giving the boy a gentle but definite shove, out of his path. He tried to walk on.

"Hey!" Zovich shouted at no one and everyone. "You saw it! He *nishiated* force against me!"

The proper word, of course, was "initiated," and the charge false—stupid, in fact, since Zovich had grabbed Berdan first. However, Berdan realized with a renewal both of weariness and fear, logic wouldn't stop trouble from coming now.

"Youbetcha, Kenjon!" The third boy, Stoney Edders, grinned wide with conspiratorial glee, and Berdan realized the whole thing was a put-up job. This was where they'd been headed all along.

"We saw it! He *nishiated* force!"

just deepened the mystery which hung about him like the cloak he now swept off his hip, exposing an enormous old-fashioned projectile pistol belted around his waist.

"You wanna play grown-up games," Forsyth continued in the stunned absence of any reaction from the four boys, "you better be ready to pay grown-up prices."

"Ah . . ."

A nervous Geeky Kehlson glanced from side to side at his companions who'd each taken a step backward. He imitated them, but not before they'd taken yet another. As they all took a third step, they turned and seemed to vanish from the park.

It was, it seemed to Berdan, a day for miracles. He opened his mouth to speak, to thank the old chimpanzee for his help, but Forsyth held up a palm and shook his head, letting the cape he wore drop back over the handle of his pistol.

"Get yourself some hardware, son. Somebody like me mightn't always be around."

Forsyth turned. Transformed once again (a final miracle for the day, not quite as wonderful as the previous two) into the fragile, elderly being he'd always seemed before, he hobbled back to his bench, picked up his paper, and sat down.

Still wordless, Berdan watched Forsyth for a moment. Breathing deep, he continued along the sidewalk and out of the park. He was careful, this time, to watch for anybody who might be waiting, out of the old warrior's sight, to get even. Pondering the chimpanzee's practical-sounding advice—as opposed to the philosophy his grandfather forced him to follow—he made his way, more rapidly than before (and with more confusion), toward the nearest transport patch.

He walked straight into its tingling embrace.

And disappeared.

few weeks ago the old man had reversed himself, allowing Berdan to go to work for Mr. Meep.

Thus Berdan knew he was in serious trouble of some kind—again—when he saw Geanar, a harsh, preoccupied expression on his big face as always, standing downstairs just outside the doorway membrane, hands on his hips, waiting.

"There you are!"

For a brief, comforting moment, Berdan entertained a fantasy: he saw himself turn around and merge into the patch again, letting the transport system take him somewhere, anywhere, as long as it wasn't here. But he knew this would only postpone what was about to happen. He had no place to go and would only have to come back again. Besides, his grandfather had seen him exit the patch, which, of course, was what he'd had in mind, waiting for him in the doorway.

"Where've you been?" Geanar's grating voice carried across the narrow street, little more than a wide sidewalk in this neighborhood. "You took your sweet time getting here!"

Berdan glanced around, self-conscious. At this hour not much traffic moved along the street, but one or two passersby had glanced up at the sound of Geanar's voice. Worse than anything he could think of, Berdan hated to be hollered at in public—it was embarrassing—but he was helpless to do anything about it. He'd tried talking to his grandfather about it, only to be told to mind his own business. At that, he'd been lucky not to have provoked a more violent reaction.

He hurried across the street, hoping the old man would lower his voice as he came nearer.

"Berdan Geanar, the next time I send for you, you'd bloody well better not dawdle!"

The last thing Dalmeon Geanar might have been called was inconspicuous, even when he wasn't shouting. He was large, with huge hands and a belly to match hanging over his belt, if he'd been wearing a belt. He wasn't even wearing pants, but instead,

terrupted him. Hoping against long experience that he'd be allowed to finish for once, he rushed on.

"Geeky Kehlson and Crazy Zovich and Stoney Edders wouldn't let me—"

"Thorens Park?"

Berdan wouldn't have thought it possible, but Geanar's complexion grew even redder. His painful grasp tightened even further on the boy's tender shoulder.

"What were you doing in Thorens Park? There are a dozen patches between Meep's greasy spoon and there! You think I went to all the effort of calling so you could waste your time—and mine—loafing with your no-good friends?"

Only three such patches existed, in fact, and the "effort" in question consisted of thinking about calling him at Mr. Meep's. But pointing this out wouldn't make Berdan's situation any better. (Nor would trying to wriggle loose from Geanar's grasp; he'd tried it before, and knew the hard way.) Appealing to facts and logic never accomplished anything but making the old man madder.

Inside Berdan, an unbearable mixture of anger, pain, and contempt boiled over. "I wasn't loafing, and they're *not* my friends!"

Still holding Berdan's shoulder between a thick forefinger and a thicker thumb, which felt to the boy like titanium clamps, Geanar bent down and peered into his grandson's face. He wasn't shouting anymore. He'd fallen silent. His lips were compressed into a short, straight line. His color had faded in an instant from reddish-purple to white. Berdan knew this was going to be a bad one.

"Defy all precedent and tell your grandfather the truth, you ill-conceived little barbarian." Geanar's roar had diminished to a far more terrifying whisper.

"You've been fighting again, haven't you?"

It was clear to Berdan that, without any evidence or justice, the old man had just convicted him of what was considered in their household the ultimate

tion near one wall at floor level caught Berdan's eye. It was the housemice, out to play when the people were away. In a well-kept modern building, they wouldn't have been seen at all.

Perhaps the humidity slowed them down. This room, the kitchen portion of it, his grandfather's bedroom, and the bathroom were filled with potted plants, hundreds of them, which the old man tended, watered, fertilized, and misted every day. Their apartment looked like a jungle, felt and smelled like one, as well.

Berdan had never understood his grandfather's obsession. He didn't dare so much as touch the old man's plants, as green things seemed to die a horrible death in the presence of what Geanar called his "black thumb." In the boy's opinion, which had never been consulted in this or any other matter, plants belonged outdoors. He preferred animals, although he'd never been allowed to have one, warm things which could move around, with a personality and eyes to look back at you, things which were maybe just a bit unpredictable.

As usual, what could be seen of the apartment's windows through all the greenery had been left adjusted to display the brightest, busiest, most crowded intersection aboard the *Tom Edison Maru*. To anyone unfortunate enough to be without an implant, they'd have appeared to be nothing more than blank sections of the walls. Although Berdan had heard it was considered smart, in certain better off neighborhoods, to have real windows with real glass looking out onto real streets, he liked these windows better: they could look anywhere.

His grandfather needed the feeling of other people around him, even though he never seemed to like people much. Berdan liked them well enough, he supposed, but preferred to let the windows of his own, one hundred percent plant-free, bedroom give him a computer-enhanced view of the star-brilliant blackness through which *Tom Edison Maru* quartered in her endless journeying. This was another transgres-

tion, in popular theory, which could be passed on to succeeding generations) which had been responsible for the slow death she'd suffered at the hands (or claws or tentacles) of primitive aliens during the exploration of a new world. This was all the detail the boy had ever been given. His grandfather wouldn't talk about it. Berdan didn't even know what planet had been involved.

"Pay attention!" A huge, rough hand landed on Berdan's shoulder and rattled his teeth again. "If you'd stop stargazing and listen for once, you might make something decent of yourself!"

"Yes, Grandfather."

But all the time, the boy was thinking to himself, *Just like you, Grandfather?*

Attempting to escape the public outrage that had followed these events, Dalmeon Geanar had fled his post aboard another great ship of the fleet. Taking his son, Berdan's father, MacDougall, with him, he'd arrived at the *Tom Edison Maru.* The story had traveled with them, however. The son, who according to the stories had gotten along no better with his father than Berdan did now, had published notice of legal separation from his surviving parent.

With all his heart, Berdan wished for some part of MacDougall Bear's courage. He even wondered if some truth mightn't be discovered, lurking in this theory of hereditary cowardice. That his father, according to all accounts, hadn't suffered any such affliction was something he failed to consider, along with a possibility that his grandfather, having learned from a son independent enough to run away, had brought the grandson up fearful and helpless.

In any case, when he hadn't been much older than Berdan, MacDougall had left home, struck out on his own, found work, and began to educate himself. He'd even rejected his father's name, adopting the one his mother had been born with: Bear.

But tragedy is a relentless hunter. Little more than a decade later, MacDougall and his beautiful wife Erissa had come to their own untimely end, re-

separate implant-activated padlocks connected a series of stout cables wound around it. Squeezing out through the front door, it bumped against the sill.

"Be careful with that thing!" Dalmeon Geanar ordered. "Can't you see it's fragile? And watch out for my pseudophilodendron! Hurry up, or it'll be late!"

"Take it easy, doc," the gorilla answered. "There's a shuttle leavin' every hour on the—"

Geanar purpled, and only in part, Berdan knew, at mention of the small ships which the old man, as a former Broach technician, trusted less than the instantaneous transport they were built to establish between the planet and *Tom Edison Maru.* Whatever Grandfather was up to, it must be urgent for him to consider using a shuttle.

"Who do you think you're talking to? I'm not paying for your lip! I'm paying you to do as I tell you!"

"You ain't payin' us enough, doc. Cool down or you can do the muscle work yourself."

As they vanished through the membrane, the human partner shook his head and muttered "Sheesh!"

When they'd gone, Geanar strode through the open membrane of his room, expecting Berdan to follow. When he did, what he saw on the bed astounded him further. The old man, who never went anywhere, had his suitcase—for as long as Berdan could remember it had lain on a shelf in the closet between two bags of plant food, gathering dust—half filled with clothing and other personal items.

"I'm going on a business trip." Geanar made it an announcement without looking around at his grandson. At the same time, he folded a brand-new smartsuit, an item of apparel Berdan hadn't even known his grandfather possessed, and laid it atop the other items in the suitcase.

"While I'm gone—no, you won't be going with me— you'll have to take care of yourself. When I get back, things will be different. At long last I'll *be* somebody. Somebody important! We can move out of this dump and get a decent place to live in a decent sector of the ship—maybe even go back to Earth! I'll hire you

CHAPTER IV:
Happy Birthday, Berdan

The silence was deafening.

It took Berdan a long while to regain his composure. From experience, he knew it would be even longer before he'd assimilated everything that had happened today.

So far today, he corrected.

It seemed to him he'd never been able to experience the right emotion at the right time, only realizing afterward, sometimes as much as several days, he'd been happy, satisfied, or proud of something he'd accomplished. Now, everything on which he'd ever based any sense of normality had been reversed within the space of minutes (a half-conscious reference to his implant told him it was just coming up on noon) and he wondered, and in the same instant regretted having thought to ask, what else could happen to him before this day was over.

He didn't want to know.

Shaking his head, he took the three short steps necessary to take him through the artificial jungle of the apartment into its cooking area—contiguous with the living room and too small to be described with any accuracy as a kitchen—and peered into the refrigerator. Removing a bright-colored plastic package, the contents of which would have upset Mr. Meep, he popped it into the microwave. With a glance back toward the greenery-filled living room area and

progress if curiosity weren't a stronger force, in particular in fifteen-year-old boys, than culture. His congealing lunch ignored now on the temporary coffee table which wouldn't go away again unless its load were removed, Berdan swallowed his conscience and stepped through the still-dilated door membrane into Dalmeon Geanar's bedroom.

The die, as someone had once observed in somewhat similar circumstances, was cast.

At first Berdan stood motionless in the precise center of the small room, both hands thrust into his smartsuit pockets in a final, futile gesture to his ruptured scruples. The place was just as filled with hanging and potted plants as the area outside, and it was difficult to take it in with a single glance.

The bed had made itself, of course. The closet had retrieved and hung up whatever clothes his grandfather hadn't taken with him and seemed to be busy cleaning them—Berdan could hear a faint ionic hum from that direction. The windows on all four walls and the ceiling were blank, unprogrammed, the place devoid of any clues he might have hoped to find. Curious or not, the boy couldn't bring himself to open any of the dresser drawers—it didn't occur to him this was a strange place to draw the line, having once violated someone else's privacy—but he wondered where the big crate had stood. In the daytime, his grandfather almost never closed his bedroom door, but Berdan hadn't noticed it before this.

Maybe it had just arrived today.

Casting aside everything he regarded as decent behavior, Berdan opened the closet. On first inspection, as the cleaning hum died, no trace remained of the crate, although room enough was left for it. Everything was as it should be, neat, spotless. Overhead, coiled tight against the ceiling, the closet's retrieval tentacle gleamed in the dim light. Whatever their other failings, the housemice, golfball-sized cyberdevices similar to the tentacle, had done a commendable job wiping out their natural prey, the dustbunny, along with every other trace of dirt

tem, broke into a seventh level museum last night, apparently for no other reason than stealing a worthless, possibly dangerous memento of a decade-old scientific experiment which culminated in two deaths.

"Some folks just have ghoulish interests, I guess," Captain Burris Griswold asserted, claiming the break-in at Spoonbender's Museum of Scientific Curiosities, 22-24 Ponsie Street, Sector 270, was the first crime of its kind in the eighteen years he has been a security subcontractor aboard *Tom Edison Maru*. Expressing doubt the thief would ever be caught, he said there is "only so much sentient beings can do" and, in his words, "Griswold's is a property-protecting company, not in the business of collecting people, not even crooks."

Contacted at home, museum owner A. Hamilton Spoonbender would not respond to questions. Infopeek has learned that the stolen object was an experimental smartsuit, centerpiece of the museum's collection, originally developed by Laporte Paratronics, Ltd. and considered a failure after two researchers were killed during its testing.

For more Infopeek info on the Spoonbender Museum, Griswold's Security, crime aboard *Tom Edison Maru*, or the experimental smartsuit's tragic history, request Sidebar Series 2335. An additional 50 gr. AG charge will be added to the accounts of nonsubscribers.

A handful of stillpix had been published with the story: a holo of the front of Spoonbender's Museum (to Berdan it looked more like the pawnshop it also claimed to be); a candid three-dimensional portrait of Captain Burris Griswold, a tough-looking character whose expression sent a shiver down the boy's spine; one of A. Hamilton Spoonbender himself, whose flamboyant moustache and eyebrows curled up on the ends; and a picture of the smartsuit itself, still in its tall, transparent display case—about the same size as his grandfather's crate—looking as if it

was just a fifteen-year-old kid, after all, without any money, in all probability without any job, and without a leg to stand on where his guesses were concerned. A surmise, he appreciated (and in this he was ahead of many adults), even based on the strongest of feelings, wasn't the same as a fact.

Knees stiff, Berdan began to get to his feet. Maybe the best thing was to tell Mr. Meep about the whole thing. Maybe the old chimpanzee could tell him what to—

"Ow!"

Berdan had hit his head again, this time on the underside of an overhanging closet shelf. All sorts of odds and ends which had been stored on it began tumbling down onto his surprised and unprotected shoulders. The worst, amidst a hailstorm of rolled-up socks, sweaters, underwear, and spare shoes, was a sizable box, upholstered in thick, coarse-grained reddish leather, which struck him on the upper arm, leaving what he was sure would be a bruise. If it had fallen on his head, he thought, he'd have been knocked out cold.

Being as neat as he could, Berdan began putting everything back. The box—more of a briefcase than anything else—was fastened shut by means of some sort of powerful, hidden catch. The thing possessed no visible outer locks nor any hinges. He shrugged and was just about to slide it back in place, as well, when he noticed, above the handle, a name embossed in the leather and inlaid in gold:

MacDougall Bear

This had belonged to his father!

Beneath the swiveling luggage handle a metal plate, two inches on a side with a shallow, bowl-shaped depression in its center, had been set into the leather. Having absorbed most of what he knew, like all kids everywhere, from adventure stories his implant summoned up for him, he recognized an old-fashioned thumbprint-activated lock. Which meant,

happens—not likely at this point—he can hold onto it until you're old enough to learn to use it wisely. Your mother and I have made other provisions, financial ones so you'll never have to worry, but this is personal.
We both love you.

Your father,
Mac

The tissue-plastic crinkled, loud in the empty room, covering up other noises Berdan wouldn't have wanted anyone to hear. After a while he wiped his eyes on a sleeve and began unwrapping whatever his father's briefcase contained.

Inside the thin plastic lay, rolled up upon itself, a wide, heavy belt of the same color and texture as the case. Along its length were flap-lidded pockets, at least a dozen of them, containing one unfamiliar artifact after another. Berdan recognized an inertial compass and a big, unpowered folding knife.

The belt hadn't been cut straight, however, and it supported more than just a series of utility pockets. From the right-hand side, where the leather had been formed into a gentle, low-hanging curve, an open-topped holster had been suspended.

And in the holster, dark-finished and deadly-looking, rested the bulk, inert at present, of an enormous fusion-powered Borchert & Graham five megawatt plasma pistol.

were human in origin or which Berdan recognized. From behind the small counter at the window, a wrinkled, ropy, carrot-colored periscope with a black faceted lens the size of Berdan's fist, peered out at the boy. *"Sorry, we're closed today—deliveries at the rear!"*

Berdan dropped his overnight bag and the briefcase and slapped both palms over his ears. It felt as though someone had stabbed his eardrums with a pair of icepicks.

"Oh, I'm *extremely* sorry!"

What had been an excruciating high-pitched squeal now became a normal-sounding human baritone, almost a bass. The orange periscope rose with a series of jiggling motions until Berdan could see it was rooted in what looked like an old-fashioned army helmet, painted fluorescent pink. From beneath its bottom edge a fringe of rubbery gray-green protuberances undulated as the freenie they belonged to, and whom they served as feet and hands, climbed up the ramp built for it behind the counter, crossed the surface to the window bars, and stuck its periscope neck and glittering eye out from between them.

"Please forgive me sir or madam, I was just speaking to my mother on the 'com and forgot to downshift frequencies. I hope I haven't caused you too much discomfort."

Sir or madam indeed. Berdan was indignant. Any member of a species boasting seventeen sexes—he wondered which of its parents the creature counted as its mother—ought to be able to tell the difference between a mere two.

"That's all right," Berdan answered the freenie. "I, uh . . . I'd like to speak to Mr. Spoonbender."

"Wait there a minute," the freenie suggested. "We really are closed today—burglarized last night and taking inventory for insurance—but I'll see if the boss is busy."

The alien trundled toward the ramp, stopped, and looked back at Berdan, its voice now a whisper. "Ac-

in permanent death-struggle with those of a Sodde Lydfan rotorbird. Scattered about the huge room Berdan could make out at least a hundred semifinished projects, tools and parts lying on bench tops amidst plastic sawdust, metal shavings, and scraps of other materials.

Even above the odor of Spoonbender's meerschaum, Berdan could smell the streaked and grimy coffee machine which stood in the corner with the sandgator and the rotorbird. Here and there, at one bench or another across the vast, disorganized, and cluttered shop, looking less like workers and more like tornado victims searching the rubble for their belongings, Berdan saw half a dozen beings of assorted species. Everywhere he looked, coffee cups stood in various conditions, some full, some empty, some in between. Several were full of peculiar, fuzzy orange mold.

"This delightful creature . . ." When they'd made their way to the middle of the workshop, Berdan's host removed the pipe from his mouth and took the gauntleted arm of a short, plump, cheerful looking woman with a welding mask pushed back onto the top of her head. ". . . is my lady wife, Vulnavia Spoonbender."

"*The* Vulnavia Spoonbender?" Berdan inquired, taking the small hand she offered and shaking it.

"*Touché*—one point for the kid. And, speaking of kids, these young ruffians . . . " Raising his voice to a shout, Spoonbender pointed to a pair of boys a year or two younger than Berdan, busy carving a fifteen-foot totem pole with chain saws. ". . . are my sons, Shep and Curly."

The chain saws stopped.

As one, the boys protested, "Aw, c'mon, Dad!"

"Very well, as you like it: N.O. Spoonbender and N.T. Spoonbender, esquires. May I also present my esteemed associates, Miss Nredmoto *Ommot* Uaitiip, Mr. Rob-Allen Mustache, and Mr. Hum Kenn, whose acquaintance you've already made."

Berdan was somehow certain "N.O." and "N.T."

don't you—Great Albert's Ghost! *That's* where I heard the name! *The* MacDougall Bear—and you'd be his son?"

Berdan hadn't had a chance yet to straighten them all out about his name. On the other hand, what did it matter? He was MacDougall Bear's son, after all.

He nodded. "That's right, Mr. Spoonbender. I heard about the burglary and thought I'd come and see . . ." He wasn't sure what he'd come here to do. He didn't want to accuse his grandfather outright, not to a third party.

One small idea in the back of his mind had pushed him through the door: selling his father's pistol, so he could pursue the old man and discover the truth. But he'd never done anything like this before. He wasn't sure whether he wanted to or not. The pistol was the one thing his father had managed to leave him.

He spoke. "I was raised by my grandfather, Mr. Spoonbender, and never knew much about my father and mother. I came to find out more, especially about how they died."

Mrs. Spoonbender frowned, as if she were thinking about her own sons growing up without mother or father. With an abrupt movement, she flipped the dark-visored helmet into place and went back to her welding. Berdan heard her sniff back a tear behind the mask.

In the embarrassed silence that followed, Ommot offered Berdan a cup of coffee—it seemed to be the tribal custom in this place—which, being as polite as he could about it, he refused.

"The Brightsuits . . ." Spoonbender mused, appearing to be speaking more to himself than to anybody in the room. "It's said three of them were created to begin with, prototypes, years in the making. Two of them were destroyed, and the last, which I bought as surplus, had been built as an emergency backup. They all possessed certain features which, at least in theory, would have allowed instantaneous transport through space—"

they'd been afraid to try further dismantling), and sold the suit for scrap prices, demanding a waiver of liability from the purchaser.

Spoonbender had bought it for exhibit in the museum he maintained—and which Berdan hadn't yet seen—next door to his workshop. The boy also suspected the man harbored dreams of trying to solve the technical riddle it presented—or had, before the inexplicable theft of the otherwise worthless artifact.

"Somehow," Berdan told Spoonbender when the story—what there had been of it—was finished, "I'm going to recover that suit, for personal reasons. That's why I'm here."

Berdan felt bad, not telling his new friends about his grandfather but thought it just as well. He was beginning to believe the old man must have been desperate to make some kind of mark in a universe where he felt he was regarded with contempt, and, whatever else he might think about it, it was private family business. Let them think his reasons had only to do with his mother and father.

"The trouble is, Mr. Spoonbender, I've never done anything like this before. To tell the truth . . . " He thought, with that same old sinking feeling, about the failed desserts at Mr. Meep's. "I've never managed to do much of anything at all, and I don't know how to start."

"Upon the incomparably beautiful planet of Sodde Lydfe where I was born and reared," Ommot suggested, a ripple passing through her fur, "a backwater podunk of the quintessential order and a terrific place to be *from,* we've a saying: *'Grot yt siidaikmo ad yt hai's, dit yt nydviimon, niivdoef eth nrais.'* "

"Which means?"

A suspicious expression dragged Spoonbender's bushy eyebrows into near-collision.

"Roughly translated," Mustache replied, " 'If at

ting the leather run through his hands. At one point he stopped, with a brief grunt of surprise.

At long last, he spoke. "Son, I know I'm going to hate myself for this in the morning, but what you really need is a recharge and some gun-handling and shooting lessons. You've no need at all to sell this fabulous weapon or to borrow money from anyone."

Berdan moved closer. "How's that?"

"Observe . . ." Spoonbender ran a thumbnail along the top of the belt, where it parted and the lining peeled back of its own accord. Between the layers, a long row of large coins had been concealed, each over a quarter of an inch thick, at least an inch and a half in diameter, bearing the portrait of the heavy-bearded historic president every Confederate recognized, and made of solid gold.

". . . twenty-four, twenty-five, twenty-six, twenty-seven! Two-ounce gold superlysanders, minted by Gary's Bait & Trust late in the last century. Relatively rare and hardly the most convenient of denominations, but, my boy, you're a wealthy man!"

Berdan's mind reeled. Just thirty seconds before, he'd been destitute and desperate. Now, he realized two things. First, he owed a great deal to the honesty of this peculiar individual, who might have bought his father's pistol for a song and never told him about the gold. Second, MacDougall Bear hadn't been altogether trusting of Dalmeon Geanar and had supplemented the financial arrangements he and Erissa had made through the old man for their son's future.

Reaching out, Berdan plucked three coins—as close to ten percent as he could get—from the pliable lining which, over the years, had molded itself to the metal disks.

"Mr. Spoonbender, you've given me valuable information, and I believe I owe you—"

Spoonbender assumed a melodramatic posture and let his eyes flash with theatrical anger. "Sirrah, you impugn my motives, insult my integrity, dishonor my ancestors, and . . ."

CHAPTER VI:
Hot Pursuit

Not quite two hours had passed since Dalmeon Geanar had departed the small apartment he shared with his grandson in the wake of a large, mysterious crate.

To Berdan, left on his own for the first time in his life, it seemed like an eternity.

He'd spent some uncounted amount of time trying to decide whether his suspicions about his grandfather—that the old man had stolen the fabulous Brightsuit—were justified, more time figuring out what to do about it, and almost an hour in the congenial bedlam of Spoonbender's Museum and Friendly Finance Company.

Now, having succeeded where Diogenes had failed, and having obtained some useful advice from the honest man he'd found, Berdan was on his own again. Making his way toward the Broach depot on the lowest level of the ship, he wished he felt up to wearing the broad, heavy gun belt which, instead, he still carried in the briefcase where his father had left it for him over a decade ago. The trouble was— and it seemed to Berdan this typified everything he was going through at the moment—he knew nothing about operating the Borchert & Graham plasma pistol it had been built for (he couldn't even tell if the thing was loaded, let alone shoot it), and didn't have any time to learn.

self, they nestled into her flattened underside, blending into her outline and contributing the output of their tachyon lasers to her own.

All along Berdan's path airlocks holo-decorated with advertising urged him to hire the services of this or that shuttlecraft. He walked right by without noticing a thing.

Away from the mother ship, the shuttles left behind great inverted bowl-shaped empty docking bays in her underside. The largest of these auxiliary craft, seven of them in all, carried seven smaller craft in the same manner. Each of these tertiary vessels housed seven even smaller vessels, and so on, from the giant starship down to scouting machines which carried a single passenger.

It never occurred to Berdan, who'd grown up in the Confederacy, to wonder why a civilization with something like the Thornes Broach needed starships and auxiliaries. While a Broach could reach out from its anchor point in time and space to place people and cargo anywhere within a range of several light years, it was difficult, dangerous, and expensive to do so without a second, receiving station at the destination end. Most of the smaller spaceships were equipped, as their primary function, to carry and install such a receiving station.

Others did preliminary exploration.

The driving machinery—no more than a turn of phrase, since it contained not a single moving part—of the *Tom Edison Maru* herself was to be found on this lowest level, along with everything required to maintain her environment and accomplish her mission: circulation pumps, filtration plants, chemical refineries, and fusion reactors. In this sense, the ship was rather like any of the vast industrial cities of Earth or her better developed colonies.

This was the one portion of *Tom Edison Maru* where one was always aware—unless one was a fifteen-year-old boy on a desperate mission of his own— he was aboard a starship, itself a giant machine, pulsing and throbbing with more pent-up energy

"Well," he told her, "it's like this: my grandfather took one of the shuttles, but . . ." Berdan hesitated, uncomfortable and aware he was treading on someone's rights to personal privacy.

Again.

The girl, accustomed to some hesitation on the part of certain of her clientele, was patient with Berdan, although she might not have been if she'd known the reason. "Yes?"

"Er, I thought I'd surprise him, that is if I could find out where he went."

The girl looked at Berdan in an odd way, but without, he hoped, too much suspicion. "Your grandfather, you say."

"Yes, ma'am. Dalmeon Geanar, Lindsay Arms Apartments, Number Two-C, Five Eighty-seven Claypool Street, Sector Twenty-nine, Fourth Level. My name's Berdan Geanar.

"I'm his grandson."

He realized, just as the last three words came out of his mouth, how stupid and redundant they must have sounded. The girl smiled an apology, although it wasn't her fault, Berdan thought, he couldn't think of anything intelligent to say to her. Girls always had that effect on him, even in the best of circumstances. He'd long ago decided he incurred less risk keeping his mouth shut, although this policy wasn't going to be of much help here and now.

"Well, if you want to surprise him, I guess there isn't much point in calling ahead, is there?"

"No," Berdan agreed. "Can I find out who went down in what shuttles earlier—about two hours ago?"

The girl shook her head. "To tell the absolute truth, the shuttle traffic wasn't very heavy this morning. This is just a stopover, if you know what I mean, a milk run, not a popular or important destination. Just see how few Broaches are being used this afternoon."

In fact, Berdan had noticed he had the whole huge place almost to himself.

"However," the girl continued, "I'm sorry I must

"Hmm. I believe I know what you mean. Local color. Are you absolutely sure—"

"Yeah, I'm sure. I wish I weren't."

"All right, let me see." For a moment her beautiful blue eyes acquired the absent, searching expression typical, on occasions, to implant users. She was looking something up or consulting with somebody. Berdan, a lifelong implant user himself, noticed but saw nothing odd about it, since he often looked the same way himself.

Her eyes focused.

"Okay, Talisman, at the south pole, is definitely the place you want to start with—not the town itself, mind you, which, it says here, is a perfectly respectable place—but a sort of suburb down there they call Watner."

Again the pause and the absent look. "Get yourself a gun, since you're not wearing one, leave most of your money aboard ship in a nice safe bank account, and keep your spare hand on your wallet, anyway."

"Thanks," Berdan replied. "I already have too much gun, which I don't know how to use, will probably need all my money down on Majesty, and, as for spare hands . . ." He held his up, both of which were full of luggage.

The girl smiled and shook her head. "Well in that case, take any of those Broach booths over there, deposit three silver ounces, and tell the implant receptor where you want to go. In theory, you'll come out in another booth, exactly like that one, at the other end."

"Thanks," Berdan replied. "Especially for the 'in theory.' I really needed that. Uh, do you happen to have change for a gold two-ounce superlysander?"

"Nothing's ever easy with you, is it?" She accepted the massive coin from Berdan, one of the three he'd offered Spoonbender, handed him his change— a great deal of it—and a plastic company token.

"Something they won't tell you in the tourist brochures because it's bad for business: watch out for

CHAPTER VII:
The Sea of Leaves

It was like being dropped into a room full of bright green ping-pong balls.

Berdan didn't sink far into the leafy morass, but without any place to plant his feet, nowhere he could push with his hands, he found he couldn't stand up again. Instead, all he could do was lie on his back, helpless and floundering.

Overhead, the sky of Majesty was a bright and cloudless blue. Everything else, as far as he could see (which, lying in this position, wasn't far) was an endless ocean of green, every possible shade and hue and saturation. Scattered here and there among the leaves were clusters of small, rather disappointed-looking pale green flowers and clumps of berries of about the same size and color.

The air was hot and damp.

All about him wafted the smells of lush vegetation, the sharp tang of the leaves and stems he'd broken, the sweeter breath of new growth, the richer, loamy odor—swampy, like that of just-picked mushrooms—of whatever lay beneath. He dreaded sinking into that organic-smelling darkness, never to resurface.

According to everything he'd seen and heard, the mossy biosphere of Majesty would tolerate no other plant life, but existed in ready symbiosis with countless animal organisms living on or beneath its sur-

Well, whatever it had been, he'd given it all the time in the world to get away—

—or to squiggle down the back of his suit!

At this spine-chilling thought, Berdan squirmed, sinking deeper with every movement, until the leaves began closing over his face like living quicksand.

Panic threatened to seize him.

He refused to let it.

Again he forced himself to relax, taking deep breaths (after all, he thought, they might be his last, and he might as well enjoy them), and spread his arms out again.

It didn't work.

This stuff wasn't water, or even quicksand for that matter. Even when he settled down, stopped sinking, he didn't float back to the top. It was hopeless. He wouldn't be able to hold still and would go on sinking, deeper every minute, until—

"Screeeeegh!"

"Yaaaaaaagh!"

Behind him, something much larger than whatever creepy-crawly he'd worried about earlier bellowed and reared up over his head. Berdan screamed at the same time. A shadow fell over his face. Huge and black, it blotted out the sun.

The first, most hideous and lasting impression the thing made on Berdan's mind was of *legs,* thousands upon thousands of legs. The horror rearing above him seemed to be composed of nothing but restless, wiggling, spike-joined legs.

It was at least as wide as Berdan was tall, about the same color as the vegetation, and smelled like a stack of dinner dishes which had been left in the sink for a week. What he could see of it was twice his height. More, perhaps: he realized, in some remote part of his mind, it must be a great deal longer than it appeared to support the portion standing up among the leaves. Either that or it was built like a bird, a great deal lighter than it looked.

He noticed the jaws, similar in construction to the

It felt just like the seminaked tail of a large, energetic rat.

"Hey!"

He still hadn't managed to open the briefcase. To Berdan, it felt like a nightmare he suffered all the time where he tried to run faster and faster, only to stay in the same place. Before he could unlock it, the case was snatched out of his hand by what appeared to be a small, eyeless blue-gray velvet-covered snake.

"Hey, cut that out!"

His other bag was wrenched away.

Something—some rough pair of somethings—seized him by both smartsuited ankles.

He'd just become aware of this development, when another pair of blue snakes, identical to the one which had taken his case, wrapped themselves around his wrists, pulling against one another until he was stretched flat on his back again.

He began to rise out of the leaves.

In this position, staring, whether he wanted to or not, at the sky overhead, it was difficult to see what sort of thing or things had grabbed him and his possessions. He was grateful that a snakelike object like the ones around his wrists and ankles hadn't also wrapped itself around his neck. The multiple whistling noises were so loud by now they hurt his ears. They seemed to arise from all around him. With a growl of anger and frustration, he twisted his neck— the attempt was painful—and was rewarded with a peculiar sight.

Each of his outstretched limbs was being held, four or five feet above the ocean of leaves, by a creature which seemed strange, even to a boy used to associating with aliens (and other nonhumans) every day. While it was their limbs—soft-textured, tapering tentacles which had reminded him of velvet-covered snakes—he was in contact with, the principal thing he noticed about each of them was the eye.

Each had only one, but, somehow, it was enough.

It was as if a three-legged starfish had been formed from plasticine modeling clay, the legs stretched as

He also wondered how it was that the taflak, with just three skinny tentacles apiece, somehow managed to keep their heads (a figurative turn of phrase at best) above the weeds, when he himself, with four much broader limbs, had settled toward the center of the planet. The half dozen natives escorting his bearers were even doing cartwheels—revolving limb over limb, while at the same time passing the stubby, long-bladed spears they carried from the tentacle about to hit the "ground" before them to another high above their plump, triangular torsos.

As soon as he'd asked himself this question, he knew from the information his implant had absorbed back aboard ship that the taflak were of much lighter construction than human beings—it was the same idea he'd had about the many-legged monster. For millions of years they'd evolved in this environment, among this infinity of leaves, and the ends of their tentacles splayed into hundreds of fine-stranded supporting "fingers," each over a foot long.

An unassisted human or a simian, without such support, would sink into the denser growth to a depth in the biosphere sufficient to immobilize him, where he'd die of suffocation or starvation (dehydration being inconceivable) if he wasn't eaten alive first by the voracious wildlife rumored to infest it. Berdan's smartsuit might have let him survive—at least until things got around to the "eaten alive" part—but it was old, worn, and had never been subjected to a test like this. He'd never even been able to get the hood, which lay limp and useless across his chest, to fasten around his head in the proper manner.

He could sure use that Brightsuit now, he thought, if he had some ham and eggs.

More than a hundred foolhardy individuals, his implant told him—Confederate, not native taflak—disappeared without a trace on this planet every year.

Watch out for the rats.

His implant also informed him the monstrous beast which had tried to eat him earlier was a "can-

be in the kind of equatorial jungle where the race evolved—as the can-can. Also, since they employed fire and were obvious toolmakers and users, they required a firmer, more stable base for their activities than the vegetation itself provided.

Thanks to this reasoning and the information he'd absorbed, Berdan wasn't surprised to be carried up a long, sloping ramp onto a large raftlike structure, woven from the dried stems and branches of the single species of plant life on the planet. No doubt its invention had been a major milestone in taflak history.

Atop the woven platform—to Berdan the pattern of its weave resembled some of the checked or shredded cereals he was accustomed to eating for breakfast—from squat beehive-shaped domes of the same material, emerged dozens more of the odd sentients, the taflak equivalent of women, old men, and children, eager, he thought, to see what the hunting party had brought home this time.

Berdan wasn't certain he liked being a trophy.

He was a great deal less happy when, instead of setting him on his feet, now that the security and solidity of the village platform lay beneath them, they paraded him about, pausing at each and every hut so the inhabitants could examine him on their own doorsteps with a giant glassy eye and curious tentacle before his bearers passed on to the next dwelling and the next exhibition. This happened several times before Berdan's patience was exhausted.

"Okay, okay! Enough's enough!"

This time, he struggled much harder than before, flailing both his arms, jerking at the imprisoning tentacles, kicking his legs. The brochure inside his head had been correct in one respect: the taflak were light of build. Although close to his size, he guessed the largest of them weighed no more than thirty or forty pounds, about the weight of a medium-sized dog. Under different circumstances he'd have been waving them around like laundry on a wash line.

The implant, however, had understated their

CHAPTER VIII:
Pemot

Flames crackled.

The whistling of the natives grew shriller.

Smoke began rising about the giant cauldron, stinging Berdan's eyes and making him sneeze and cough, as the taflak holding him in the pot backed away from the fire.

Maybe they burned easier than humans, thought the boy, his implant offering him no information on the subject. For whatever reason, it appeared they thought their efforts to restrain him were no longer necessary, that he wouldn't pass over or through the barrier of flame which now surrounded him like a wall. Maybe they'd just never had a dinner impolite enough to get up and walk away.

Well, if that's what they think, they're wrong!

The circle of spear bearers standing around him showed no inclination to move, one way or another. The choice between frying pan and fire, Berdan thought, was easier to make than he'd ever imagined, and the forks—those pointed spears—weren't even worth worrying about. Keeping an eye on them nonetheless, and wincing a bit as the fine hair on the backs of his hands began to singe and crisp away, he seized the edge of the pot, put one foot over, and—

"I say . . . " These words were followed by a series

Like crabs, Berdan knew, lamviin wore their skeletons on the outsides of their bodies instead of inside like human beings, porpoises, gorillas, and what-have-you, although, unlike crabs, they wore a thin layer of skin over their exoskeletons.

The remarkable difference, setting them apart from crabs and every other creature which had evolved on Earth, was that they were trilaterally, instead of bilaterally, symmetrical. Cut a human or a chimp down the centerline (a depressing thought, considering the situation Berdan found himself in now), and each half would be a mirror image of the other, whereas a lamviin would have to be cut into thirds.

With humans, almost everything was in pairs: two eyes, two ears, two arms, two legs, and so on. With lamviin, it was trios or triads or whatever they called it: what started out as three stout legs (or arms, with lamviin it was pretty much the same thing) where, crablike, they joined the carapace, wound up as nine smaller appendages by the time they reached the ground, having branched somewhere in the middle, terminating in delicate hands with three opposing fingers.

Or toes.

When Berdan's ancestors had climbed down out of the trees, their next great accomplishment had been getting up off all fours and standing erect. The lamviin feat was walking on just six of their branched limbs, holding the remaining three up in front ("front" being defined as the side on which three limbs were being held up) to use as arms. It didn't matter which three. They were inclined to swap off now and again. Berdan, always fascinated by extraterrestrials, had read somewhere that showing a habitual preference in this regard was considered to be the lamviin equivalent of bad table manners or sloppy posture.

Somewhere, some poor little lamviin's grandfather was hollering about that right now.

He also knew, beneath the rubbery protection of

to the bedrock, genuine—if unexplored and tantalizingly unexplorable—surface of the planet."

Having nothing to say, Berdan said nothing.

"Doubtless," it continued, "you now find yourself speechless, if not at my statistics or with gratitude at my sudden and fortuitous appearance, then certainly in surprise and indignation at this outrage which has been perpetrated upon your person. So was I, when they first did this to me, whereas they—" The traces of curl were gone now from its fur as the lamviin indicated the entire raftlike village around them with all of its inhabitants.

The image came to Berdan's mind (not from his implant but from his imagination) of this overcivilized being flailing around, crablike, in the taflak boiling pot, and he had to suppress a snicker. Did lamviin turn red when they were cooked?

"They all think it's bloody marvelous, frightening the tourists out of their wits, so they'll flock back to watch their friends being frightened the next time."

"You mean—" Berdan, just becoming aware he was dripping wet, had managed to produce two words. Part of the problem was that all of this was beginning to strike him as funny.

"Precisely, my dear fellow. It's their idea of a joke."

"Grrr!"

It hadn't been a real growl but something halfway between a tooth-chattering shiver and laughter suppressed, not just for the sake of the lamviin's feelings, but because Berdan was afraid it was the beginning of hysteria.

"My sentiments—" The lamviin had misunderstood the noise Berdan had made. "—exactly." It sighed.

"On the other hand, I suppose, these things are culturally relative. Some people are tone-deaf, some are color-blind, and, then again, especially in the view of the taflak, who fancy themselves colossal jokesters, half the universe is humor-numb."

its eyes arranged they way they were, it didn't need to move its head—its body—to follow the boy's gaze around the village. Either this young human was most resilient or the storm had yet to break.

Berdan shrugged—a cold, wet, squishy gesture—and it was this and a certain amount of relief after twice thinking he'd been about to die a horrible death, rather than the lamviin's weak puns or quizzical expression, that broke his self-control.

He chuckled, caught himself with a hand over his mouth, and chuckled again.

It was like an uncontrollable fit of hiccups. He looked from the dozens of taflak surrounding them, to the lamviin in its odd getup, to the oversized cooking pot behind him, down at himself (grass-stained and soggy), and began to laugh, collapsing against the pot—still cold, since the fire had just lasted a few seconds—until he couldn't breathe and tears were streaming from his eyes.

Once opened, the doors to hysteria couldn't be closed again, and it began to spread. Before he knew it, the lamviin had collapsed beside him, its fur curled tight, its leg-nostrils making peculiar hooting noises and wheezes, independent of one another.

He'd bet lamviin *could* sing in harmony with themselves, Berdan thought, and the idea—like everything else at the moment—seemed too hilarious for words. It started him laughing all over again, until he thought he'd suffocate. He put one arm around the creature as they both convulsed with laughter.

It, too, had tears in its eyes.

All three of them.

The taflak, hundreds of them now, closed in around the laughing pair, their whistling louder and higher pitched than ever. The whole silly thing, Berdan thought, had been some kind of ritual ordeal, a ceremony, a test. They liked somebody who could take a joke, and in all probability ate anybody who couldn't.

One of them—one of Berdan's original rescuers or

CHAPTER IX:
Marooned

". . . and the word 'cannibal,'" Pemot insisted, "wouldn't have been a correct technical description in any case. Unless you insist upon taking the Pansentient position that all intelligent lifeforms are members, ethically, of the same species."

Somewhat resembling an octopus on a beach ball, with his legs draped all around its circumference, the lamviin rocked back on the inflatable hassock which served his kind as a camping stool. Not far away, in a small ceramic holder with a perforated cover, burned a stick of *kood,* a gentle incense which seemed to energize and relax him, in the same way a cup of tea might for a human being.

"Mmph." Berdan replied from around a bite of his Sodde Lydfan sandshrimp sandwich, "It's not a bad way to look at things, is it?"

"No." Pemot leaned over and inhaled the *kood* smoke. "No, I suppose it isn't, at that."

Night had fallen over the Sea of Leaves.

Following the taflaks' practical joke "ceremony" and a resulting outburst of hysterical laughter which had ended, for Berdan, in a deep and dreamless sleep (the boy had been carried again, this time unconscious, to this hive-shaped hut which the taflak had loaned Pemot), he'd recovered his belongings—his own zippered Kevlar bag and his father's gun case—and had discovered among the Sodde Lydfan's ra-

"I see, sort of a folk joke."

"Isn't that what I—oh. Another attempt to demonstrate that you've a humerus?"

"Why not? It seems to have worked with the taflak. What did you do when they threw you in that gigantic pot?"

"That was different. In the first place, the climate here is much too cold for me, and I rather enjoyed the unexpected warmth, however damp the experience. My people, as you may be aware, have a considerable aversion to water. Also, it was what I was here to investigate. I pretended to go along, although I confess, it didn't really strike me as funny until I saw it played on you."

Berdan snorted. "Isn't that the point?"

"Why, I—" Once again the Sodde Lydfan scholar pulled out his peculiar three-sided notebook and started up furiously scribbling. This time he was at it for a long while. His stick of *kood* burned out. Berdan finished eating, tidied up—the chore amounted to nothing more than stuffing plastic bags into one another and placing them where they could quietly and safely self-destruct—pushed aside the hand-loomed curtain which covered the door and peered out into the night.

If Majesty possessed a moon, it had either set or wasn't up yet. Outside the hut, village and sea were as dark as Berdan, a city boy, had ever imagined anything could be—like the inside of a closet, he kept thinking, with the door shut tight. His grandfather had punished him that way on more than one occasion: locked him in a closet. It was the stuff many of his nightmares were made of.

Inside, they had more than enough light. His new friend had come equipped for ten taflakological expeditions, and an item he'd scrimped on least was portable fusion-powered lamps. Four were burning now in a space not much larger than the closet which the outdoors reminded the boy of. In addition to the Sodde Lydfan and the human, the hut was jammed

materials from specialized portions of the single plant species on the planet."

"That's interesting. Such as?"

"Such as that rather large pot with which we both share an intimate acquaintance, the pride and joy of the entire village. It's made from a clay which, for some obscure biological purpose the plant life accumulates, and which the taflak concentrate from a certain berry it produces at a certain time of the year."

"They also have some metal—spear points and so on. Or do they trade for that?"

The taflakologist tried to lift his limbs where they joined his body, imitating a human shrug.

"A spot of both . . ." His tone changed. "Do you know, my friend, what with that cannibal joke and what happened afterward, your sleeping so long, I just realized I've never learned your name."

It was true. Pemot had introduced himself, under a rather memorable set of circumstances, but Berdan, being busy at the time, had failed to return the compliment.

He shook his head. "The name's probably mud, by now, back aboard *T.E.M.*—a family name, guilt by association. The taflak won't have to extract it from berries any more."

He stood, stooping in the low hut, and stretched out a hand to the Sodde Lydfan. "Berdan Geanar, late of the *Tom Edison Maru* by way of good intentions and a malfunctioning Broach: slapstickologist, itinerant incompetent, avoider of the sentient condition, at your service."

Pemot laughed his hooting laugh. "I say, Berdan Geanar, well spoken!"

He extended the middle of his three hands to be shaken.

"I'm most pleased, sir, in the extreme, to make your esteemed acquaintance. And what, if I may venture to inquire, brings you to this chilly garden planet?"

Letting go of the other's three-fingered hand, Ber-

uld have been a kid's word against an adult's, and,
matter where you come from, you should know
w that works—or maybe you don't. Because no-
dy would have believed me, Pemot. Anyway, the
hole thing was about my family, so I decided it was
p to me. Unfortunately, I was just a tad late, and I
ad the rotten luck to choose a malfunctioning
Broach."

"I see. Has it occurred to you your grandfather
might have taken certain measures to assure he
wasn't pursued, once his act of theft had been discovered?"

A light dawned in Berdan's eyes. "What do you
mean?"

Before he spoke again, a deep breath whistled
through the lamviin's half dozen nostrils. "Well, insofar as I understand it, and I assure you that I'm
no technician, the Broach itself—a man-made hole in
the very fabric of space-time—is a simple device, re-
liable, difficult to tamper with, and almost invaria-
bly functions perfectly."

The boy's chuckle was grim. "Yeah, well if that
were true, I wouldn't be here to give you an argu-
ment about it."

Pemot blinked. "Indeed. On the other hand, measures sufficient to preclude pursuit might involve
something no more complicated than reprogram-
ming an implant-receptive computer, changing a
Broach's paratronic characteristics a microscopic
amount—which, of course, would throw its calibra-
tion off by thousands of miles."

Berdan nodded and blinked at his friend. "I get
t—or it got me—and my grandfather used to be a
Broach technician."

Pemot began to blink, changed his mind and tipped
is entire body first down and then up. "Anyone at-
mpting to follow his illicit rendezvous via commer-
al Broach, would, upon requesting any destination
th one Dalmeon Geanar in mind, find himself
anded in the most primitive area of an already
mitive world, a hemisphere from where he had

mind of a small mystery I've encountered, and I was
wondering whether there might be a connection. I
rather doubt it."

The boy raised his eyebrows. "Try me."

"Well, you'll recall my saying the taflak are rather
less primitive than they may appear. I'm inclined to
identify with them in this regard. My own people,
you see, while more advanced (we'd just begun using—and, I fear, misusing—nuclear fission) when
your people discovered us, were still rather backward by comparison to the Confederacy, and we've
had a deal of catching up to do."

"And so?"

Pemot turned a hand over, a human-looking gesture which was Sodde Lydfan, as well. "And so, not
too very long ago, as an experiment, I determined to
introduce the taflak to the benefits of science and
undertook construction of a pair of simple amplitude-modulated radios—transmitter and receiver—
such as my people began with. I built the receiver
first, so as to have something with which to test the
transmitter. Imagine my surprise when I discovered
someone here on Majesty was already making use of
this almost-forgotten technology."

Berdan's shrug was more successful than the lamviin's had been. "Well, why shouldn't they?"

"Because, my friend, in the first place, no one of
Confederate origin has used simple electromagnet-
ics, let alone amplitude modulation, for well over a
century. Paratronics, employing the same principles
as the Thorens Broach, has too many advantages."

"Okay," Berdan suggested, "if it's so simple,
couldn't some native genius have invented radio on
his own?"

The pair of eyes Berdan could see (the third being
around the circumference of Pemot's body) blinked,
something the boy would learn to interpret as a nod.
"In the beginning, I suspected as much. But three
reasons come to mind to doubt it."

With one hand he indicated a finger of another.
"First, the inhabitants of near-polar villages in con-

intended to be, alone and friendless. With any luck—
if your grandfather refrained from interfering with
other traffic—a considerable time might pass before
the sabotage could be detected."

"Which shoots down the idea of rescue. I figured
they'd be spraying folks to the wrong destination all
over this crummy planet, and a full-scale search
would be on."

"Not," replied the lamviin, "if your grandfather
was at all clever."

"And so here I am. Stuck."

"Quite so, my friend, albeit as a highly probable
result of your grandfather's treachery, rather than
by bad luck or any incompetence on your own part.
I doubt whether he realized he'd be stranding his
own grandson. And yet, knowing what you know,
you remain the one individual in a position, however
hopeless it may be, to interfere with his betrayal of
the Confederacy."

"What do you mean?"

"That 'the Hooded Seven' is a name for a conspir-
acy not entirely unknown among the lamviin."

"Oh yeah?"

"Er, 'yeah.' And that it represents the greatest
threat to civilization as we know it."

form. Here he sat down, somewhat stiff, leaning back against the woven wall of the lamviin's hut, trying to think, but not knowing where to begin.

Berdan hadn't learned yet: sometimes it isn't necessary to begin all at once. Sometimes just sitting in the quiet darkness does as much for someone in pain and confusion as any train of logic or course in therapy. Berdan sat, watching the night, smelling the sea on the soft, alien breeze, feeling things.

Before long, Pemot was beside him.

Something else the boy didn't know: the edge of the village platform could be a dangerous place at night—can-cans were the least of such dangers—which was why the taflak were all tucked safe into their huts, dreaming whatever dreams they dreamed. The lamviin, however, although not much older than Berdan in terms of his own culture, was wise enough not to lecture, but just to keep an eye on the boy and on the sea, his pistol unobtrusive but ready.

Time passed. After enough of it, the boy turned to the Sodde Lydfan scientist. "Pemot, are these Hooded Seven guys really a threat to civilization as we know it?"

Inwardly, the lamviin grinned to himself, once again admiring his new young friend's resilience of character. Outwardly, his fur crinkled, the appropriate overt expression for the emotion, but in the dark this was invisible.

"I thought you'd missed that. Yes, Berdan, some of us lamviin believe so: my family, one member of it in particular. The threat they represent is vague, but, I fear, real. And, somehow, all the more terrible for its vagueness."

The boy strained to see his companion's face in the dark, until he realized it didn't matter. "What do you mean?"

"I . . . Berdan, I think the best course in the circumstances would be to tell you a story—history, in fact—the full details of which haven't been known to

heroic and terrible wound acquired in the defense of one of our colonial frontiers, he'd even, upon one occasion, been put to court martial—and acquitted, I hasten to add—for mutiny.

"During all this time, however, throughout each of his many and varied adventurings, Uncle Mav had esteemed himself first and foremost as a seeker of scientific truth and general wisdom, in particular within the realm of ethical philosophy. Having begun as an humble, pragmatic, and, in the main, self-taught investigator of life's mysteries, large and small, in the end he attracted the devotion of many younger lamviin of all three genders whom, in angry tones, he refused to let call themselves his students or, even worse, his followers.

"And at last, when he'd become an old lam indeed, with painful, creaking joints and the fur thinning upon his carapace—at a time when a final, cataclysmic conflict between the rival polities threatened inevitable destruction, not only of everything lamviin regard as civilized, but of all life upon Sodde Lydfe itself—he endeavored to make practical use of everything he'd learned, everything he'd himself created, in order to forestall disaster.

"It had long since occurred to Uncle Mav that the impending catastrophe, like most of the military and diplomatic events preceding it, was an affair, not so much between the peoples of the Empire of Great Foddu and the Podfettian Hegemony, as between their respective rulers. He'd come to believe the pathway toward genuine peace lay not in the direction of negotiations between leaders and mutual disarmament (this being, at the time, the avenue most acclaimed and heralded by those of conventional mentality who, sincere or not, professed to love peace and abhor war—one which, as an individual, let alone a former soldier and policeman, he distrusted), but in the severest possible reduction of the power, the importance and prestige of the rulers themselves.

"For uncountable centuries past, the untram-

Lydfan atmosphere for hundreds of thousands of years.

"The final battle had just begun when an astonishing thing happened. High in the air above both fleets, an impossible, gigantic, gleaming hemisphere materialized. Broadcasting on all frequencies, it ordered hostilities to halt, and, when not obeyed, employed powerful, surgically-precise beams of energy to blast holes through certain of the warships—and only the right ones—destroying the nuclear explosives they carried, allowing their crews time to repair or abandon them, and ending Sodde Lydfe's first and last atomic war.

"Of course your Galactic Confederacy had discovered us. An initial covert survey team had measured the international situation, recorded and translated Uncle Mav's broadcasts. Not certain what to do about it, if anything, they'd sent for the starship *Tom Paine Maru,* which stopped the war (although debate still rages in certain quarters—Confederate, not Sodde Lydfan—whether it was ethical to interfere at all). Aided by his friends and family, a Confederate commando broke Uncle Mav out of prison. Afterward, as the Confederacy's liaison with the Fodduan government and royal family, he helped make the peace—this second chance he'd won for us, all unknowing—a thing of permanence.

"Now I've not inflicted this long and tedious story upon you without a purpose. During the aftermath, certain parties, neither Earthian in origin nor Sodde Lydfan, approached my Uncle Mav on the quiet with a curious proposition. Warning him of hidden imperialistic intentions on the part of the Galactic Confederacy and pointing out—they were correct in this—his own great popularity among all lamviin everywhere on Sodde Lydfe, they offered to place him in unanswerable power over the entire planet and to help it win free of all external interference.

Being far more interested in seeing his philosophical ideals realized—and, remaining the same inveterate seeker of truth he'd been in his youth, desiring,

planet, having had, when I came to this place, specific scientific goals in mind, rather than a timetable, and having made, on that account, no particular arrangements for my return to a more civilized—"

Berdan's jaw dropped, and a look of betrayed astonishment swept over his face. All of this was lost on the lamviin in the darkness, but the boy's tone made up for it.

"Nothing doing! I came here with a specific goal in mind myself—finding a thief and getting some stolen property back—and I'm not leaving until—"

Pemot raised a hand, which he had to place on the boy's shoulder to interrupt the flow of angry words.

"Come, come, Berdan. Let's be realistic. Far be it from me to point out the obvious: you're an immature human—a mere fifteen-year-old boy—pursuing a dangerous and perhaps impossible objective better left to the regular security—"

Berdan shook his head. "Okay, Pemot, if that's the way you feel, I can do without your help. Go ahead with your scientific goals, and I'll get on with what I have to do! Just lay off the fifteen-year-old-immature-human stuff and try to stay out of my way, that's all I ask!"

He set his mouth in a hard line intended to control a trembling lower lip, folded his arms across his chest, and turned his back on the lamviin. A longer silence followed this time, during which each being was busy readjusting his thoughts about the other, one, perhaps, less accurate in this than the other.

Pemot was the first to speak. "I believe, my friend—if I may still call you thus—I may have been misled about your civilization. Aren't all of the most cherished myths of humanity concerned with returning from someplace you didn't want to be: Ulysses and Ithaca, ruby slippers and Kansas, the Shire, back to the future, all of that?"

Berdan was a while replying. "Would we be cross-stitching the galaxy in thousands of starships, many built to stay out forever? Would our stories have been written at all? Haven't you noticed they're all about

CHAPTER XI:
The Gossamer Bomber

"Very well, then." Pemot pushed the curtain aside as he and his human companion reentered the hut. "I recognize when I've been vanquished, if not, perhaps, by superior logic, then at least by arguments which satisfy my sense of the fitness of things. That being so, we're obliged to take stock, make plans concerning what we—"

"We?" the boy asked the lamviin. "What's all this 'we' stuff, all of a sudden?"

"And why not, friend Ber—Mac, er, Bear? Am I not also a member, albeit a new one, of the civilization which is threatened by the crime you seek to set to rights? Don't I also have, if not an obligation, then a right to act toward the same end?"

The boy took his place on the floor, this time in a reclining position. Pemot settled onto a large air cushion, substituting for a traditional lamviin sand bed.

"Well, I—"

Pemot threw all three hands in the air. "Of course I do! How can you even question it? It's indubitable that you require my assistance. Whilst I, xenopraxeologist that I am, shall learn as much from you, I assure you, as you'll ever learn from me. Besides, as Uncle Mav's fond of saying, 'the game's afoot!'—you know, I've always wondered what that means."

"The way I heard it—" the boy chuckled "—the First Wave colonists were all cranks."

"Your comedic successes with the taflak have gone to your head, my boy. Where was I? Whereas more modern Confederate hovercraft work quite well on this planet, too."

"That's nice. The point?"

"Am I putting you to sleep? The point, my endoskeletonous young friend, one even I hesitate to put forward, is that before we can avail ourselves of any such transportation, we must first contact either the old colonists or the new. And we possess no means of accomplishing that except walking, Shanks' *watun*, to the poles."

"What?" Mac sat up straight, awake. "You mean in that whole pile of junk of yours, you don't have any telecom equipment?"

The lamviin's furry covering undulated, the Sodde Lydfan equivalent of a shrug. "Why should I have required it? I am, to my certain knowledge, the one representative of my species here at present upon Majesty, as much an alien to most Earthians as are the taflak. Rather more so, I daresay. What's more, I'd planned—and still do, for that matter, thanks to recent events—to be on the move."

The boy leaned forward. "But what if you needed something, Pemot, like your own kind of food or medical help?"

"I've no elaborate requirements. Supplies least of all, having suffered an heroic course of anti-allergic carapacial infusions on Sodde Lydfe before coming—my insides still itch where they can't be scratched, whenever I think about it—and being able to ingest taflak victuals without ill effect."

Mac shook his head, wishing he'd taken similar precautions. To this point, he'd been nibbling on Pemot's civilized supplies and a few things he'd brought from home himself. It might get pretty hungry here on Majesty before this was over.

"At my uncle's advice," the lamviin continued, "I replenished my crop with brand-new, oversized

"Yeah, well you can start by telling me how it works—and whether or not it's loaded."

"Dear me, I'll give it my best, by all means. What sort of weapon is it, anyway?"

Mac leaned over to snag the briefcase. He opened it and extracted the weapon.

"It says here, right on the barrel: Borchert & Graham, Ltd., Tempe, Ariz., N.A.C.—M247 Five Megawatt Plasma Pistol Rev. 2.3—Before Using Gun Read Warnings in Instruction Manual. Except I didn't find any. What's plasma?"

"Someone, my dear fellow, has neglected your education. Plasma's a fourth phase of matter, as in: solid, liquid, gas, *plasma*. I caution you, I'm no physicist. And it seems peculiar to be explaining this to someone born into the culture which taught me and mine, but there you are. Subjected to temperature so extreme even the word no longer means what it did, atoms disassociate—molecules are unable to form— and lose their electrons, acquiring a positive charge which is used, like a handle, to concentrate and direct them.

"Do you, er, follow that?"

Mac didn't answer.

He'd fallen asleep.

Mac pushed the door curtain aside and emerged into the sunlight, where Pemot seemed to be talking to himself.

"Well, that, I believe, does it. I can't take everything, but I never intended—yes?"

"How are we going to travel with all of that?"

Mac pointed to the pile of possessions, as tall as its owner, heaped up on a transparent plastic ground cloth in front of the taflak dwelling Pemot had occupied.

"All of what?" Pemot protested, sounding hurt. "There isn't that much of it, is there?"

Some justice could be seen in the complaints of both sides. The lamviin had managed to compress what had seemed an entire hut full of equipment

"Ku Emfypriisu Pah, what do you suppose that is?"

Mac squinted until his eyes watered. He was rewarded with the sight of what at first appeared to be a large, slow-moving bird approaching the village. As it neared, the boy changed his mind. The bird's wings were stationary and transparent, as was its body, once it had come close enough for him to see.

It was an aircraft, silent and transparent.

"It's a museum piece, Pemot, some of your First Wave colonists, coming to pay a visit."

"If so, it would be most unprecedented. I gather the first Majestan colonists left Earth, wishing to have as little to do with other 'races'—insignificant morphological variations within your own species— as possible. Thus they've never associated with—I say, what *are* they about in that contrivance?"

Mac shook his head, and began to laugh. "Why, they're pedaling, Pemot. If I hadn't seen it myself, I wouldn't have believed it. That's why we didn't hear it coming. The plane's powered like a bicycle."

Mac was correct. He and the others could see now that the aircraft's occupants had their feet in stirrups, cranking a long chain which drove a pair of big, transparent, slow-moving propellors at the rear of the machine. As it neared the village, the huge control surfaces tilted, and the aircraft's altitude diminished from the several hundred feet at which it had first been seen to a few dozen.

"Are they planning to visit us?" the lamviin asked. "Where are they going to land that thing?"

"How should I know? It sure looks fragile."

In another few moments, it was over the village.

"I say, *not* First Wavers—those are chimpanzees at the pedals, aren't they? What do you—MacBear!"

Mac shoved Pemot behind the hut. A chill had gone down his spine as he caught a glint of metal.

"Not just at the pedals—they also have guns!"

Mac had just gotten the words out, when the sizzle of plasma pistols filled the air, joined, a fraction of a second later, by the alarmed whistling of hundreds

Mac followed Pemot's instructions. What he assumed was a pilot lamp under the rear sight gave off a dull glow. A faint hum could be heard from somewhere inside the mechanism.

Several more chemical-powered gun blasts assaulted the boy's ears. Pemot had at last managed to connect with the aircraft. Small holes had appeared in its forward-mounted control surfaces. Meanwhile, its occupants had stopped shooting, seemed to be having trouble turning or had decided to turn the other way.

Sighting along the barrel, Mac observed, "I'll bet they didn't expect us to defend ourselves!"

A ball of plasma, glaring like a miniature sun and impossible to look at, flashed past them and hit the platform, which burst into flame a few feet away.

Pemot ducked—too late, for the shot had missed him by at least six feet. "Do you call this defending ourselves?"

Mac's hands, wrapped around the pistol, had begun to shake. He took a deep breath—trying not to choke on the smoke which enveloped them—and squeezed the trigger.

A pale beam of reddish light reached out toward the aircraft, followed by a belch. A sickly yellow blob of energy wabbled along the beam and glanced off the plane. Anticlimactic as it was, it was enough. One wing caught fire and began to burn. Its occupants furious at the pedals, the machine turned away from the village, trailing smoke, and sank lower with every few feet of distance it gained.

Both the boy and the lamviin heard it hit the moss with a faint crunch, some distant yelling, and—

"*Yeeeegh!*"

Mac turned to Pemot.

Pemot turned to Mac.

They both spoke at the same time.

"Can-can."

The boy grinned, and, from the texture of the lamviin's fur, guessed Pemot was grinning back. All at

CHAPTER XII:
Middle C

The plasma gun and firebomb attack on the taflak village didn't delay Mac and Pemot long.

They'd already been prepared to go, for the most part, and their belongings were undamaged by the ill-fated and futile aerial assault. Also, they felt the sooner they left, the safer the Majestan friends they left behind would be. Since he understood the language, Pemot took care of the farewells.

These, given the nature of their hosts, were somewhat lengthy. The taflak, like many sentients at a similar point of development, tended to hold ceremonies on any excuse. Mac made good use of the time, however, since, at some point during the battle, his subconscious mind had put his previous experience in the moss together with the sight of Pemot's sand-sled, and given birth to an idea.

Receiving permission from the lamviin, he spent the hour Pemot was away fussing with sheet plastic and plastic-covered wire. Soon, wearing the "moss-shoes" he'd "invented," with his father's pistol heavy about his waist, his bags consolidated and strapped onto his back by the handle straps, Mac preceded the lamviin down the ramp and was about to step off into—or, he hoped, onto—the moss, when a whistle shrilled behind them, and Pemot touched the boy on the arm.

"A moment, if you please, MacBear."

seldom found in such a state. They were, most often, a blur of motion, and their preferred method of travel was the one Mac had already observed, cartwheeling from tentacle to tentacle, which may have been the only kind of travel that made sense on the surface of the Sea of Leaves and a great way to get around, but made the taflak difficult to examine in any detail.

Just as mankind's remote ancestors (typified by starfish or sea urchins) had been constructed on a five-sided plan, from which bilaterality had later evolved, these creatures displayed an underlying trilateral symmetry, but had, in recent geological history, begun evolving into something approaching the human arrangement. In this rare, motionless state, they tended to balance on one of their three appendages, each resembling a woolly but close-trimmed splay-tipped elephant's trunk, with the other two, used for manipulation, stretched out and upward, making the entire creature look something like a round-bellied letter Y.

The great transparent taflak eye, transfixing the entire creature, could see backward, forward, and to all sides at once—a biological necessity on the perilous planet. Being large and symmetrical, Mac had already seen it, although he'd missed the faint lacework of blood vessels (at least he thought that was what they were), thin nervous and supportive connections visible through its ultra-transparent fluid between the black-surfaced ball floating in the center, constituting pupil, retina, and brain, the velvety surrounding flesh, the three peripheral tentacles, and the vital organs contained in their bases.

Where the high-pitched whistling and chirping talk came from, Mac never did discover.

"You know, I realize we both took the community joke like real sports and all, but it's nice of Middle C," the boy commented to Pemot, "to come see us off this way."

The lamviin's fur crinkled, the equivalent, Mac had begun to learn, of a chuckle. "On the contrary, my young conclusion-jumping friend, the fellow in-

built, filtered, and shielded now against accidental
emissions, and equipped with a directional loop antenna. They'd strike out for the north pole, they'd
decided, hoping to run into a First Wave crawler or
a Second Wave hoverbuggy which might save them
part of the otherwise epic journey. But, along the
way, they'd attempt to triangulate on the enemy's
amplitude-modulated signals.

"Suits me," Mac answered, his terseness hiding
his feelings. "The more the merrier."

Without another thought about the risks involved,
he stepped off onto the moss. And onto a road, in a
figurative sense, which would take him halfway
around the planet.

"Onto" turned out to be the right word, after all.
Mac's moss-shoes performed even better than he'd
expected, although, like the snowshoes they resembled, they were tiring to use at first. They made his
ankles and the inside muscles of his legs sore for
several days but did their job of distributing his
weight over a far greater area, allowing him to stride
along right beside his six-footed, eighteen-toed lamviin friend, instead of sinking into the sea.

If Pemot held back for the boy, he never said so.
Of course they both understood—and appreciated—
that Middle C was crawling along on his figurative
hands and knees, compared to his normal rate of
travel.

Early the first day, Middle C advised them both,
through Pemot, that they'd be encountering far less
dangerous wildlife than might otherwise be the case,
just because three of them were traveling together,
rather than one or two. The native was too polite,
Pemot told Mac, to mention that two of the three
were so clumsy on the moss they scared everything
away within several square miles.

"Although, given a chance," the lamviin wondered aloud to his human friend, "how well would
Middle C do in the Neth, the great central desert of
my native Foddu?"

Nevertheless, Middle C scouted ahead, rolling back

first place, grew weary of the sameness of the blue sky above and the green Sea of Leaves below—gray and black respectively when it happened to be raining, which was often. The horizon was as flat as that of any ocean, and as featureless. He began to think a person could go insane if he were exposed to enough of this emptiness.

Another thing bothering Mac, although he'd never have admitted it to Pemot, was that the cerebrocortical implant he'd grown up using all his life was as good as dead. While it contained plenty of information—not only about Majesty (most of it incorrect, he'd discovered, or not detailed enough to be useful), but everything else he'd ever recorded and hadn't afterward erased—he hadn't laid in a stock of movies, books, or music suitable for a long, wearisome trip. Not much of what he did have was entertaining or even interesting. No object he could see around him, not even the lamviin's hoard of technology (having come from a far less sophisticated culture), would respond to the device. No information channels operated on Majesty to be received.

Squaring his shoulders, he told himself to be a man. This was just like camping out. Like doing without indoor plumbing (which happened to be the case, although one's smartsuit took care of such things when it worked right). Maybe he could program his implant to teach him the languages of his new friends. Maybe he could learn a new word of his own language every day, from its internal dictionary. Maybe he could memorize the cube roots through four figures. In any event, he'd either get used to it or put up with it until it was over.

He spent a good deal of time wishing it was over.

Every day, Middle C would wheel ahead out of sight on one of his scouting missions and return with some unlikely-looking wild animal which he'd killed for them to eat. Mac admired the taflak's prowess with the spear thrower and itched to try it out himself, but was too shy to ask. Pemot would prepare the game—anything from slithery nonsentient rela-

On one cold and miserable night in particular, when they were huddled together for warmth under a plastic shelter half and couldn't sleep, the Sodde Lydfan scientist, worse off but too proud to admit it, attempted to amuse the human boy by telling him something of what he'd learned among the planet's natives.

Middle C had just left to go hunting.

". . . and so the taflak believe something more than bedrock lies at the bottom of the sea."

"Oh yeah." Berdan began to yawn—and broke it off to shiver. "Like what?"

"Well," Pemot replied, "stories seem to vary from village to village, as folktales have a way of doing, but the gist is always of an ancient culture, one which possessed great magical powers of healing, of locomotion, of flight, perhaps of mass-production (judging by legends of abundance in the Elder Days) but which, as always seems to be the case with the mythology of sentient beings, denied, defied, or defiled the gods and afterward paid the price—extinction. Everything they'd built was swallowed up in the Sea of Leaves."

Mac yawned again, beginning to feel sleepy. One advantage of rooming with a desert-planet sentient: it was as good as carrying central heating with you.

"Hey, pretty neat. Sort of an Atlantis with runaway landscaping instead of ocean water. Do you think any of these legends is worth believing in, Pemot?"

"My dear boy, as I just implied, every race of beings which attains sentience seems, at times, to regret the attainment enough to make up stories like this."

"Yeah, but—"

"Furthermore, how could they know, either about the past or what lies below? They possess no written language—"

"Yeah, but—"

"And no Majestan native—nor colonist of either wave, for that matter—has ever seen to the bottom

CHAPTER XIII:
The Crankapillar

It came from the edge of the world.

When they first saw the thing, far away on the hazy green horizon, it resembled, more than anything, a can-can on wheels. At least fifty pairs of fat, oversized, underinflated wheels were rolling, rim to rim, linked by flexible couplings. The thing slithered toward them, as sinuous as one of Middle C's tentacles.

That entity, straining to the uttermost tip of his supporting appendage—the equivalent of standing on his toes—became agitated and at first didn't seem to hear the frantic questions Pemot was asking him. At last he relaxed—although Mac noticed his grip on his spear thrower had tightened, and he'd transferred his ammunition to his other tentacle—stood down, and spoke to the lamviin.

Pemot blinked. "I was afraid of this, although I'd half hoped it would occur as well, a stroke of some sort of luck, although only time will tell whether it's good or evil."

Mac had been standing on tiptoe, one hand resting on the handle of his Borchert & Graham. "What is it?"

Pemot rummaged through the contents of his sandsled, gave his usual exclamation, and pulled out a long, glass-ended metal cylinder which resembled a telescope only until he pulled the front half away

the amplitude-modulated broadcasts. This is the location where my lines cross for the stronger of the two. The transmitter's somewhere within a few square miles of the spot we're standing upon this minute!"

"Great! And what does Middle C have to say about all this?"

"It would appear, he says, that in finding them we've allowed them to find us. They'll be a long time getting here—if here is where they're headed. They can't be going much over five miles per hour, and they're a long way away."

Mac resisted an urge to crouch down in the leaves. "Do you think they can see us?"

"My friend, these people left your home planet only sixty years ago, in 223 A.L.—1999 by the old reckoning—and, although they've had their cultural ups and downs in the subjective millennia which have passed, for them, since then—" He indicated the instrument in the boy's hands. "—I believe they're up to the simple optical technology which binoculars and telescopes require."

It was confusing, Mac thought, even when you understood it. Among other problems, the starship which first brought humans to Majesty had been blown backward a long way in time. Thus, although it seemed paradoxical, the planet was pioneered thousands of years before the very people who did it ever left the Earth. Meanwhile, for the civilization they'd fled, only sixty years or so went by.

He felt a fuzzy tentacle on the back of his hand and passed the lamviin binoculars over to Middle C, who'd become curious about them. The taflak warrior placed both tubes before his single large eye, held them first further away, then closer, made a gesture the boy was certain was a shrug, and passed them back.

Mac laughed. "Did anyone ever tell you, Professor Pemot, that you can be an awful pain sometimes?"

"Why, no," the lamviin replied, "they haven't. Why in the world would they want to do that?"

the cup from the burner and dropping some leaves Pemot had recommended into the scalding water. "Go right ahead."

"Very well. Majesty's a lost human colony, one of several hundreds founded during your people's disaster-ridden First Wave of emigration from Earth, which through a scientific failure, misplaced its victims in time as well as in space."

The lamviin began whistling, repeating what he'd just said for the benefit of Middle C.

Mac stood up to observe the progress of the crankapillar they were waiting for.

It didn't seem to have moved.

Having heard about this famous "scientific failure" before, both in history lessons and in various fictional adventure programs aboard *Tom Edison Maru*, he was disinclined to be as serious about it when it came from an alien viewpoint, however scholarly. It was interesting, however, to hear Pemot do the extra talking necessary to explain some of the concepts to a warrior-hunter of a primitive tribe.

When Pemot had finished this second time, the boy tried whistling a tune of his own. *Lost colonies—careless of them, wasn't it?*

The taflak slapped him on the back. Pleased with the boy himself, Pemot let his fur crinkle with a mixture of professorial annoyance and involuntary amusement.

"I suppose one could look at it like that. On the other hand, I'm not altogether certain they'd have cared about the outcome, even if they'd somehow known it in advance. As I'm given to understand, MacBear, times were changing on your planet, and the original First Wavers would have done anything at all to leave."

Mac glanced at the horizon—the crankapillar seemed to have disappeared—realizing it had only dropped into a slight hollow in the gentle, rolling surface. For a long while it almost seemed they had the Sea of Leaves to themselves once again. He

Mac grinned. "Yeah, I'll just bet you have. Did you tell him we've even begun to explore a few of those universes? That's what Thorens invented the Broach for, after all."

"Actually," the lamviin corrected the boy, "she invented it believing she was producing a faster-than-light starship drive, at the behest of one Ooloorie Eckickeck P'wheet, a porpoise, who was responsible for the theoretical work.

"By the way, I believe, if you'll observe now, that our friends in their absurd machine have made some visible progress. They shouldn't be too much longer."

All three strained for a minute to watch the crankapillar. They settled down again around the sled. Mac had gotten another cup of water to the boil. Out of polite reflex and mild curiosity, he offered his second cup to the taflak, who surprised him by accepting it, placing a number of his tendrils in the liquid— the level began to drop—while leaning into the *kood* smoke to enjoy that as well.

Mac shook his head. "Pemot, how come it always seems you know the history of my people better than I do?"

"Perhaps," the scientist replied, "because I come to it freshly, like any immigrant. In any case, it was neither Thorens nor P'wheet who bungled the First Wave's departure. That had been predicated upon the existence of one alternate universe in particular, different from our own, in which the Big Bang, which begins the life of most continua, either never came about—I've never been clear about this part—or came off considerably less spectacularly."

"I've heard of that—" the boy nodded "—the Little Bang universe. And the word, Pemot, is 'fizzled.' "

The crankapillar had disappeared again, which all three realized meant it was getting nearer.

" 'Fizzled,' then—this language never ceases to amaze me. In any case, ducking through it promised that one might get halfway across a given fraction of his own universe, in effect, in less time and with-

were large—seven or eight feet in diameter—manufactured from some latexlike secretion of the one plant species on the planet, inflated to the resistance of a firm foam pillow. Each open car was linked to the ones before and behind it, completing a long, semirigid structure which could negotiate any terrain.

One thing Mac had missed was that the contraption was woven out of wickerwork—also from the Sea of Leaves—with only the load-bearing portions fabricated from metal, a substance rare on Majesty, since it had to be mined at the poles.

He also observed now the inward-facing benches on each car, each occupied by half a dozen bareskinned men—something like three hundred, altogether—hunched in rows, staring into one another's sweaty faces, all the while laboring over a long, looselinked crank, which he guessed was geared to the fat wheels.

Mac was seeing his first galley slaves—for that matter, his first slaves of any kind.

He was smelling them, as well, and wishing he weren't. First and foremost, more than anything else he noticed about the machine and its occupants, was the malodorous fog of human sweat and excrement which lapped for hundreds of yards all around it, regardless of wind direction. It made the boy—and he wondered if it was affecting his companion the same way—want to throw up.

Instead, he leaned into Pemot's *kood* smoke, his inhalations deep—and grateful.

Behind each bench, between those who cranked and the soft, oversized wheels, a walkway had been constructed, also of wicker, for an ugly-looking overseer who, with his partner across from him, made sure their car pulled its own weight. They were equipped for the task: plenty of sunburned muscle and short, nasty whips, which they used with frequency and enthusiasm. As they leaned in to encourage the slaves, Mac wondered whether they ever hit each other by accident.

CHAPTER XIV:
j'Kaimreks and the Baldies

"You have our p-permission to c-come aboard!"

With a horrendous squeaking groan, followed by a leaf-scattering crash, a wicker boarding plank was tipped over the side of the rearmost section of the crankapillar, and fell at Mac and Pemot's feet, coming close to crushing them both.

Overhead, a mixed flock of transplanted Earthian scavenger birds and their membranous native Majestan competitors swooped and wheeled in hopes the ugly smell wafting from the crankapillar meant something nice and decomposed to pounce on.

"In fact, we m-must insist! Come, come, hesitation is the same as insubordination!"

Pemot muttered something in his own language which sounded insubordinate to Mac, hadn't hesitated about it, and so, the boy guessed, the relationship didn't work both ways.

Shrugging, the boy sat down on the edge of the plank, removed the makeshift moss-shoes from his feet, and, fighting his reflexive reaction to the odors around him, preceded his friend up onto the quarterdeck of the machine.

The only reason the deck wasn't dirtier was that it had been woven of open wickerwork. Debris tended to drop through, to the benefit of certain creatures who, like the birds and other things overhead, followed the crankapillar about across the Sea of

123

given the captain the opportunity to accrue a richer, thicker, more elite layer of filth.

For a long, terrible moment, Mac was certain his queasy stomach would embarrass him.

"The sidearm," repeated the captain. "Your existence is justifiable only insofar as—"

Mac gulped bile, blinked back tears of nausea, and answered between gritted teeth. "I don't think so."

"What?" The man was wide-eyed with astonishment. "Have we not explained to you that you must obey promptly and without question?"

"Yeah. So I explained to you that I don't think so. In the Galactic Confederacy, insubordination is one of our most popular leisure activities. These flamethrowers of yours are real impressive in their own small way, but they'd make a tempting target for our starship's strategic particle beam weapons." He pointed a thumb upward toward the sky, where *Tom Edison Maru* might still be orbiting, invisible at present, but a brilliant artificial star from dusk to dawn.

"Infrared sighting instruments, you know, and all we have to do is think about wanting them."

This, of course, was a lie on which Pemot and the boy had agreed while waiting for the crankapillar. Yet, if the unwashed, unshaven, and undeodoranted Captain j'Kaimreks knew anything at all about the Confederacy, he'd believe it.

"Besides—" Having practiced enough to gain some confidence with the weapon, Mac patted the handle of the Borchert & Graham five megawatt plasma pistol hanging low along his right thigh. "Before I burned to death, I'd make sure I had company. There's enough power here to reduce this crankapillar of yours, and ten more like it, to a fine white ash. Don't hurt us, we don't hurt you. Do we understand each other, Captain?"

The man with the megaphone looked up at the sky, as if for some visible portent of the *Tom Edison Maru*. He closed his eyes and shuddered, did a turn-

patient stirring in Pemot's hair. "See here, Captain . . . er—"

"j'Kaimreks," the man supplied, standing as tall as he could manage and shoving his left hand even deeper into his shabby coat. "Captain T-tiberius j'Kaimreks of the S.N.R. *Intimidator* of the N-navy of the G-government-in-Exile of the Securitasian National Republic. Our authority is metaphysically unquestionable."

"It seems to me," Mac whispered, humming through his nose, "that I have heard that song before."

Each time the captain repeated one of these phrases, obvious preprogrammed slogans of some kind, Mac noticed how the slaves—and a few of the overseers, perhaps those promoted out of their ranks—flinched, as if the lessons had been applied with liberal doses of the whip or even electric shock.

Pemot blinked, doing his best to imitate a human nod. The boy noticed the man didn't offer the lamviin his hand to shake, but he hadn't offered it to Mac, either. Given local sanitation standards, this arrangement had suited the boy.

"Pleased to meet you, Captain j'Kaimreks, I'm sure. Now, shall we discuss business?"

The lamviin pointed a finger forward, toward the naked, malodorous men who'd been cranking the Securitasian machine. At that, they were no doubt fortunate to be without clothing, exposed to wind and sun and rain, since it meant less chance to carry around the miniature zoo each of the overseers, as well as their captain, seemed to have acquired. They sat at rest now, streaming with sweat, their chests heaving. It was clear from the displeased expressions of their overseers this was an unwelcome exception to the normal state of affairs.

For Mac's part, he was glad they were all downwind.

human variants behind on
ago, these pitiable crea-
necessity to have someone
m of the social heap."
ound somebody else to pick

correct word, but you're right. I'm
to how many others—red-haired, green-
individuals, those who were too tall or too short,
fat or too thin—they exterminated before they
got around to these poor 'baldies.' "

"*Left-handed* baldies," Mac reminded him, "and
probably convicted of excessive bathing."

"Indeed," the Sodde Lydfan xenopraxeologist answered, his tone and fur texture grim. He held one
of his arms up. "Personally, I'm middle-handed, myself."

"Me, too—" Mac grinned "—*and* Bohemian."

"Indeed."

The lamviin addressed the captain. "I fail to understand," Pemot objected, moral outrage discern-
ible in his voice and in the sharp spikes of his fur,
"why any of this inlamviinity is necessary."

"That's 'inhumanity,' " Mac whispered.

"Whatever you choose to call it, it's an unneces-
sary evil. On my own home planet, Captain j'Kaimreks, until the recent perfection of steam engines,
we operated oceangoing vessels which had rotating
sails. The invention's quite ancient. The sails, you
see, were geared to a drive shaft connected to propellors.

"Now, I've had occasion to observe many times
that there's more than enough wind out here on the
Sea of Leaves to facilitate such a contrivance, so why
couldn't you—"

Shock written in his widened eyes and in the sudden paleness of his face, the captain held out his
hand, palm toward the lamviin in a desperate, defen-
sive gesture. "S-stop, you! We do not want to hear
this! We do not want our officers or c-crew to hear

CHAPTER XV:
The Revolt of the Feebs

"What?" Mac and Pemot had spoken at the same time.

"How c-could you b-be so obtuse?" asked the captain. "If we d-did as you suggest, foul alien c-creature, what would our feebs do? There would be no useful emp-p-ployment for the surplusage of them. They would have to be ah-ah-eliminated."

He peered down at the lamviin. "Do you call this humane?"

Mac looked forward, over row upon row of starving, exhausted, sore-covered feebs, and wondered if some fates weren't in fact worse—and less humane—than death. "Job security," he muttered.

"You're saying—" Pemot ignored Mac and concentrated on the captain. His speech was as deliberate as the boy had ever heard it, slow and distinct. "You're saying that the foundation on which your entire civilization bases itself is involuntary servitude?"

"We did not say this." The captain was a picture of indignant virtue. "On the contrary, extraplanetary indecency, what we have said is that their only reason for being is to do precisely as they are told, whenever they are told."

He glanced from side to side to make sure he wasn't overheard by any of his crew or officers. "Is it not so everywhere?"

Meanwhile, Pemot, watching their backs, had drawn and leveled his old-fashioned chemical-powered projectile weapon at the overseer nearest the flamethrower.

"I'd not advise it, sir."

The overseer took one look at the enormous muzzle of the gun—and at the nine-legged monster pointing it at him—and leaped over the rail into the Sea of Leaves.

The other officers followed his example.

Weapon still in hand, the Sodde Lydfan strode forward to a crude plank bridge connecting the aftermost section of the idle crankapillar to the next section ahead of it in line. His companion, meanwhile, somewhat surprised by his own actions, had crossed the deck to examine the smoking remains of the late Captain j'Kaimreks, having first put them out with a bucket of water standing beneath the canopy.

"Some pistol my daddy left me." As Mac muttered to himself, he wondered why he was unable to feel much of anything else at the moment. At least he didn't feel sick to his stomach any more. "Hey, Pemot—take a look what I've got!"

When he looked back, the lamviin—who'd lived for a while in the North American west and knew something of its legendary customs—saw, to his horror, that Mac was holding up the captain's hair as if it were a Comanche trophy.

"You put that down this minute! I greatly fear what all this violence must be doing to your—"

"My poor, tender little psyche? But it's *fake*, Pemot. It's made out of dyed moss! And, come to think of it, didn't you notice? When the captain grabbed for that blunderbuss of his, whatever it was, he did it with his left hand!"

One set of feet on the plank, Pemot paused. "No, MacBear, as a matter of fact, I hadn't noticed. However I did notice his decided stutter which, among you human beings, is sometimes thought to be a symptom of suppressed left-handedness. Captain Ti-

ground meat, breathing and sweating. His eyes were open, and the look on his face was composed and intelligent.

Overcoming revulsion, Mac bent further and shook the feeb's sunburned shoulder.

Skin peeled away at the boy's touch.

The feeb looked up. "You no officer . . ." The statement almost amounted to a complaint.

"Meebe you new cap'n? Lost tracka who's cap'n now. My body is but a tool of your mind."

He flinched.

"I will obey promptly and without question."

He flinched again.

"No!" Mac's voice was harsh. "I'm *not* the captain. The captain's dead. There isn't any captain, and won't be, ever again!"

The feeb assumed a hurt expression, sniffed, and a tear began to form in his one good eye. "No cap'n? Who gonna feed us? Who gonna tell us go an' stop? You gonna tell us?"

Once again, he cringed.

"I have no bargain with authority except to expend my life in its service."

"My dear fellow," Pemot put in. "There'll be no one to tell you what to do from now on. You're free, don't you understand what I'm saying. Free to feed yourself, or starve, or to do anything else within your power that you want to do. You're free."

The feeb didn't answer, but turned his eye back to the work-polished crank and sat motionless and dejected. Mac noticed, now, in addition to the overseer's whips and flamethrowers, each car had its own huge, long-handled brake lever.

"I don't think you understand." It was Mac who tried this time, his voice becoming a bit hysterical with the attempt. "Up there in the sky is a great big starship from the Galactic Confederacy. It won't let Securitas or any other nation-state own your body or tell you what to do, ever again. You're free—you don't have to be a slave anymore!"

"No slave in Securitas," the feeb protested. "Slav-

"Nah." The feeb sighed. "Officers don' come back, feebs hafta 'lect new officers like b'fore. Hurt head. My only reason for being is to do precisely as I am told."

He flinched, brightened for a moment and smiled. "New officers choose us new cap'n! We go! His authority is metaphysically unquestionable. My existence is justifiable only insofar as I serve him!"

A final flinch and he fell silent.

Mac straightened and turned away, his stomach not behaving well again, regained the quarterdeck aft, and began a slow descent to the ramped boarding plank.

Following his human friend, Pemot spoke first, his voice subdued and unsteady. "I must say, Mac-Bear, this is a most depressing turn of events. I suppose some social scientist somewhere knows precisely how many times one must repeat a slogan, beginning at what tender age, until it produces a state of voluntary slavery. I daresay even the late Captain j'Kaimreks was, to some extent, a victim of the process."

Mac turned. "You're the only social scientist around here, Pemot. And people worry about physicists!"

Pemot was horrified at his companion's accusation but knew enough to control his reaction. "Nonetheless, my friend, some responsibilities exist in the life of a sentient being which no excuse can justify abrogating. It puts me in mind of an old Fodduan saying: *'Eo gra fins ko vezamoh ytsa mykodsu yn tas gadsry al ys.'*"

Mac looked up from tying on his moss-shoes. "Which means?"

"Idiomatically, 'Anyone requiring persuasion to be free doesn't deserve to be.'"

The boy stood up. "Oh yeah? Well it reminds me of an old Confederate saying."

"Yes?"

CHAPTER XVI:
The Screwmaran

Someone once said "small is beautiful."

He was wrong.

There seemed to be no end, Mac thought, to low-grade technology and labor-intensive wonders out here on the Sea of Leaves. The Antimacassarite screwmaran was swifter than the crankapillar—about seven miles an hour to the Securitasian vessel's five—and had been somewhat closer to begin with, having approached unobserved while he and Pemot were preoccupied with the late Captain j'Kaimreks.

The vessel's name, which his implant supplied along with her nationality, was descriptive. The vehicle resembled the shanks of a pair of stubby, steep-threaded wood screws, counterrotating side by side, connected—to continue the nautical terminology the Securitasians had preferred—at her double bow and stern by what, for want of better words, might have been called a flying forecastle and quarterdeck. She was powered by about the same number of slaves as the *Intimidator,* not sitting at their backbreaking labors, but marching for eternity around a set of stair steps cut into the angled sides of her threads.

At once, Mac could see why the screwmaran was faster. She consisted of little more than a pair of giant propellors. No complicated gearing system

Antimacassarite culture leads me to believe it similar to my own. My greatest fear is that, despite my Uncle Mav's painstaking tutelage, I may be vulnerable to its blandishments. And this unfortunate world, like others settled by the First Wave—much like your own Earth's early history—has always been subject to cyclic collapse. It's seen countless civilizations struggle into being, blossom to maturity, waste their hard-won substance on war or internal conflict, only to pass out of existence."

"Pretty depressing," the boy replied, trying to raise one eyebrow. "Why do you stick around?"

"Because there's something here to learn, I think. Also, I enjoy the company of the indigenous sentients. Majesty's unique, for all its tragedy, differing, at least in Confederate experience, from all previous lost colonies. And, I might add, as a native of Sodde Lydfe, I can appreciate that difference."

Mac nodded. "The taflak."

"Precisely. My native Sodde Lydfe is inhabited by its own sentient population, and, *feu Pah ko sretvoh*, was never discovered by the First Wave. Although its technology's unsophisticated in comparison with yours, it's scientific and progressive, and its relationship with the Confederacy is, for the most part, as an equal."

He sighed again. "The *taflak*, haven't been left alone. The planet's first human inhabitants were intolerant, and remain so, as you've seen. Thus the taflak have been required to fight for their existence since the First Wave arrived. Themselves scarcely changing, millennium to millennium, they've witnessed the whole sorry spectacle of human civilization; and in this regard they're far from primitive, for they enjoy many clever and cynical sayings about the follies of humankind."

"It sounds to me," the boy suggested, with a close, observing eye on his friend, "like maybe you're getting a bit cynical about human beings, yourself, Mr. Xenopraxeologist."

The lamviin splayed all three hands, a gesture

immobilized crankapillar. Flamethrowers on the screwmaran's flying forecastle were aimed at the Securitasian vessel, their pilot lights flickering. Meanwhile, a detachment of several dozen figures, men and women, armed and uniformed, swarmed down the threads of the screwmaran, stopped in her shadow to tie on moss-shoes identical to those Mac thought he'd invented, and broke into two groups, each headed in separate directions.

The first group, their old-fashioned bayonetted long arms at the ready, jogged toward the crankapillar, running up her boarding plank, moss-shoes and all. Shouting could be heard—not from the dispirited and quiescent feebs, Mac thought—but no shots of any kind were fired, and he assumed the strange vessel had now been claimed by the victorious forces of nation-state of Antimacassar.

The second and smaller group, consisting of perhaps a dozen individuals (if "individuals," Mac thought, was what you called people all wearing the same clothing), approached the pair of extra-Majestan travelers and their sand-sled at a more leisurely rate, their antique weapons carried across their brass-buttoned chests, and paused a few feet away. The military uniforms of Antimacassar were charcoal gray, and much neater than the bottle green of Securitas.

Mac hoped that, somewhere in the deep sea moss, Middle C was taking this all in.

A tall, attractive, but severe-faced young woman, carrying a flap-holstered pistol, but no long arm, stepped forward, removed her cap, and saluted them. "Good day to you both, gentlebeings, I am Leftenant Commander Goldberry MacRame, Third and Security Officer of the A.L.N. *Compassionate,* a frigate of Her Imperial Kindness' Leafnavy of the Antimacassarite Government-in-Exile. Might I be so intrusive as to inquire whether you are responsible for having disabled this pirate machine, and, if so, whether you accomplished this by yourselves?"

very much to be of assistance to you, Doctor Pemot,"
she replied, "but naturally my commanding officer
will have something to say about that."

"That," Pemot answered, tipping his carapace in
yet another bow, "is entirely understandable. I assure you, whatever can be contrived will be more
than satisfactory."

Mac leaned down and whispered. "She sounds
just like you, Herr Doktor Professor Pemot. Polite
as all get-out, aren't they?" He looked up at the
woman.

She raised a single eyebrow.

"Yes," the lamviin whispered back, "as a matter
of fact, they are. Which, unless I miss my guess
entirely, means we're in greater danger than ever
before."

"I give up." Mac laughed aloud. "I thought you
were going soft on me or something."

"Not," the lamviin answered, "bloody likely."

With half of her detachment taking up the rear,
they followed the woman back to the screwmaran.

As they made their way across the open space between the two vessels, Pemot towing his sand-sled
behind him, a tremendous *whoosh!* and a wave of hot
air blasting from the direction of the *Intimidator* almost knocked them off their feet.

At the same time, they heard a hundred-throated
cheer from the direction of the *Compassionate.*

The Securitasian vehicle was soon enveloped in
flame, with greasy black smoke rising to the over-
cast above. A column of uniformed Antimacassarites
began winding, antlike, from the burning wreckage,
some carrying boxes and bundles salvaged from the
crankapillar, others towing makeshift wicker rafts
of feebs who, without moss-shoes, were helpless to
escape even if they'd been motivated to.

Quite a spectacle, Mac thought. Down deep inside,
he'd always been fond of fires and explosions but was

He followed one of the Leftenant Commander's dozen soldiers up the ladder with considerable agility—more, in fact, than Mac, following behind him, managed.

tion of the sea plants secreted it—into which they were conducted.

"Doctor Pemot of the planet Mexico!" Leftenant Commander MacRame bowed to a figure seated behind a table and indicated the lamviin.

"Mr. MacDougall of the starship *Maru.*" Again the leftenant commander bowed.

"Please allow me to present to you our esteemed commanding officer, Captain-Mother b'Mear b'Tehla. Captain-Mother b'Tehla, Doctor Pemot and Mr. MacDougall."

"Bear," Mac corrected.

"Pardon, young man?"

The white-haired old woman they'd been introduced to sat in a wicker rocking chair with a knitted shawl wrapped around her plump shoulders. She appeared to be even further overdue for rejuvenation than his grandfather. She peered at Mac with shrewd, glittering eyes through the thick lenses of bifocal spectacles.

"MacDougall Bear, ma'am—that's my name—of the Confederate starship *Tom Edison Maru.*"

The old lady chuckled. "Dearie me. We greatly fear you'll have to be somewhat forgiving of our good leftenant commander's roughshod and straightforward military manner. Without a doubt, it has its proper place aboard the *Compassionate,* as, indeed, do we all. Moreover, any inclination upon her part toward empty courtesy would be a poor substitute, indeed, for her real talents. Now, won't you be seated, Mr. Bear? And what sort of furniture would you find most comfortable Doctor Pemot?"

"A stool would do nicely, Captain-Mother b'Tehla, or I can remain standing in perfect comfort."

"By all means find the good doctor a stool, Goldberry, and have our aide bring tea in, if you will."

"Aye, aye, Captain-Mother."

Spine straight as a ruler, Leftenant Commander MacRame saluted, turned on her booted heel, and left the captain-mother's cabin, closing the door behind her.

But this is a mere peccadillo, compared to the truly heinous offense against all humanity for which, most lately, we have been pursuing him."

Mac raised both eyebrows.

"He was," the captain-mother replied to the gesture, "trafficking—although we hesitate to believe it was at the behest of his government, as uncivilized as they have demonstrated themselves to be at times—trafficking with the . . . the . . ."

"The natives?" Pemot had all three eyebrows raised, although the captain-mother couldn't see the one in back.

"Indeed"—her tone was indignant—"in an effort to enlist them in an unwholesome alliance against us."

"How innovative of him." Pemot's tone was neutral.

"The very word for it." Captain-Mother b'Tehla nodded, puckering with distaste. "Although we are certainly glad you have had a word such as that in your mouth instead of us!"

They spoke a while longer about j'Kaimreks.

Meanwhile, Mac had discovered something else. Thanks to the several cups of tea he'd had since dawn, one of his physical requirements had exceeded the capacity of his smartsuit, which, owing to its age and state of repair, had been limited to begin with. Something he couldn't quite define about the current social circumstances made him embarrassed to ask about the *Compassionate*'s sanitary facilities, and he decided to try waiting for a later opportunity.

If he could.

"And so," Pemot explained to their hostess when they'd finished discussing the Securitasians, "we drastically require transportation to Geislinger so that we may be in time to rejoin the interstellar fleet. Is it possible to persuade you, Madam Captain-Mother, to help us or to find someone who can help us?"

"Dearie me."

The captain-mother's wicker chair squeaked as she rocked it back and forth. "We're afraid this does

nevertheless had an accurate idea of the technological capabilities of orbiting spacecraft, and took pains to mask these gatherings from infrared and other kinds of detection.

As the captain-mother explained them to the fascinated xenopraxeologist, their own navigational skills were impressive, considering the primitive implements they used, and they could communicate with other vessels using flag signals, messages sometimes being relayed in this fashion a quarter of the way around the planet.

Mac's discomfort was increasing, and, at the same time, he was becoming annoyed with his companion. This old lady was just like his grandfather, whose sweetness and sunlight could transform themselves into poison and thunderclouds at any moment, in particular when his authority over his grandson was challenged.

Why couldn't Pemot see that?

"Okay then, ma'am, since we have business of our own and no intention of subverting anybody, why don't you just let us off this machine so we can be on our way? It'll get us out of contact with your precious young people that much sooner."

The captain-mother shook her head. "Dearie me. We could never accept the responsibility for so reckless a course. It is dangerous enough upon the Sea of Leaves for the fully armed and mechanized contingent we have here in the *Compassionate*, let alone a pair of relatively helpless strangers to our harsh environment such as yourselves. Why, for the sake of your own safety if for no other, we must insist you stay with us."

"Besides—" Mac stood "—your superiors might want to squeeze information out of us?"

"MacBear!"

"Sorry, Pemot, but, as far as this old lady's stock in trade is concerned, you seem to be buying out the store. I'm not. Underneath all the smiles and endearments, she isn't any different from Captain j'Kaimreks. Can't you see that?"

"Might we be so bold as to inquire," inquired the old lady, "what you are referring to?"

"By all means you may ask. But before you do, permit me to answer with a demonstration—"

The Sodde Lydfan leaned forward on his stool toward the open window, pressed two fingers to each of the nostrils beside his upraised major limb, and *whistled!* The glass panes shattered. Both tea mugs on the captain-mother's table went *tink!* as their glazing crazed, although they managed to stay in one piece.

In answer, a blurred projectile whisked up past the astonished leftenant commander through the window and thunked, quivering, into the raftered ceiling.

"Consider this a message, Captain-Mother, terse in content but certainly to the point, from our taflak friend Middle C. He and *his* friends, in fact his own tribe as well as the assembled warriors of several neighboring villages—whose territory you're violating—would greatly appreciate seeing us, alive, uninjured, and uninhibited, back down on the surface immediately."

"Or else," Mac added.

"Quite so," echoed Pemot. "Or else."

No other warriors, of course, existed. This had been one of the strategies worked out with the Majestan native before leaving him for the *Intimidator.* For a while, Mac had wondered—and worried—whether Pemot would remember it.

Captain-Mother b'Tehla's reaction was well worth waiting for. She thought of something to say, opened her mouth, closed it, thought of something else, opened her mouth, and closed it again. In the end, she seemed to find her voice.

"Snake-eye lovers! Ugh! Goldberry, take them anywhere they please but get them out of my sight!"

In ten minutes they found themselves afoot again and almost alone on the Sea of Leaves.

The *Compassionate* had turned and was speeding away at its full seven miles per hour.

CHAPTER XVIII:
Is It Safe?

Dalmeon Geanar was disgusted.

He reached up to a small, softly-illuminated panel just above his vehicle's broad, curving windshield, which even at this inhuman temperature was threatening to fog up, and turned the air conditioner knob the few remaining degrees to its last stop, trying to wring another drop of moisture out of the hot, soggy air. If the open atmosphere of Majesty was intolerable, here, just inches beneath the insulating surface of the leaves, it was a thousand times worse.

Something moist and pallid—the diameter of Geanar's wrist and with altogether too many legs for his peace of mind—slithered along the side window, leaving behind a slimy track and sending chills up the man's already sweaty spine.

The brand-new smartsuit he'd just purchased aboard the *Tom Edison Maru* didn't seem to be doing its job at all—not that he had much familiarity with such things—another failure of technology to provide properly for mankind's needs. It was, he imagined, rather like wearing an Eskimo parka in the Congo basin. Or perhaps what his eyes saw around him overrode what his body felt.

Odd, he reflected, how from the first he'd hated this planet, how it had almost seemed to hate him as well. Back aboard the *Tom Edison Maru,* he'd filled his apartment with plants of every kind, or-

was nowhere made manifest, at the behest of an un-
civil voice on his radio receiver that claimed to represent interests he wanted to do business with—
individuals he'd never encountered face-to-face, who
refused to meet him in the discreet comfort of Watner or even in Geislinger or Talisman as he'd de-
sired—only to be confronted with half a dozen shocks
all at once, any one of which could have spoiled his
entire week all by itself.

In this damp heat, he thought, it was a wonder he
hadn't had a coronary or a stroke.

The first shock had been that long, crude, snaky,
muscle-powered machine, the Securitasian crankapillar. In the beginning, when from his hiding place
just below the surface of the vegetation he'd watched
it approaching the appointed place at the appointed
time, he'd believed, despite its primitive construction, that it had been sent by the Hooded Seven. He
still couldn't bring himself to believe its appearance
was a coincidence, and wondered what it meant.

Still believing the *Intimidator* (which he didn't
know by name) represented an opportunity he'd
dreamed about and wished for all his life, which he'd
planned with painstaking care and worked ardu-
ously toward for years, he'd watched in open-
mouthed horror as the crankapillar picked up a pair
of interloping, smartsuited strangers—one human,
one alien—who'd subsequently murdered the machine's uniformed commander in a fiery blast of pistol shots and, threatening more of the same, driven
off all of the underlings.

There ought to be, he thought, some way of keeping individuals from owning and carrying weapons.

The much larger *Compassionate* had come along
and finished the job, its troops reducing the primitive moss machine to nothing more than ashes,
smoke, and twinkling coals.

Some of Geanar's initial shock had worn off. Ob-
viously the smartsuited interlopers had been, like
himself, agents of the Hooded Seven, settling some

All in all, Geanar felt he'd been patient, and expected to be rewarded for it. When contact hadn't been immediately forthcoming, still he'd waited. This was the place, all his navigational instruments indicated so, and the word he'd gotten had been that the rendezvous might occur at any time within a twenty-three hour period which comprised day and a night on this misbegotten excuse for a planet.

The worst shock of all, however, had come when Geanar saw the smartsuited interlopers being put off the screwmaran and left behind—only to be met a short while later by one of the sickening vermin who, although they consisted of little more than tentacles and eyeballs, were nevertheless rumored to be the intelligent natives of this world. He'd gotten a clear enough look at them—adjusting the windshield for maximum light amplification and magnification—as they'd climbed down the flexible ladder at the aft end of the *Compassionate.*

Incredible!

It was bad enough that one of them—another of those disgusting clumps of soulless hair and leather being treated these days by bleeding-hearted fools as the full equals of human beings—was that pseudo-scientific meddler who'd been eavesdropping on his electromagnetic conversations with the Hooded Seven. When the Voice of the Seven had warned him about that, he'd been a fool himself to hire those simian morons in Watner, instead of doing something about it himself.

He wondered what had ever become of them.

What was truly awful, almost beyond belief, was that the other interloper, co-conspirator with the hideous lamviin and revolting taflak, had been human.

And his own grandson, Berdan!

"Is it safe?"

"Hunh!" Geanar was startled by a sudden whisper close beside him which seemed to come from nowhere—until he remembered the radio transceiver lying on the next seat.

it'll remain so for some time yet to come. I'll keep a lookout as we talk, just to make sure. It's only a fifteen-year-old kid and a bemmie from some dust-bowl planet, anyway. What are you so frightened of?"

Several heartbeats went by before the voice replied. *"Earthman"*—an undertone of weariness colored the words—*"we, too, have traveled far to meet you in this place. For you, the local environment, while differing in various insignificant details from that which you would regard as most comfortable, is at least somewhat familiar. For us it is extreme, harsh, alien, and dangerous. We would find it taxing to attempt coping with discomfort, disorientation, and the necessities of self-defense, all at the same time."*

Aha, thought Geanar, the mysterious Hooded Seven reveal one more detail about themselves. He wondered how he could use the information to his advantage.

Aloud, he asked a question. "All right, granted the environmental problems, which I find quite uncomfortable enough, thank you, what do you mean self-defense? Self-defense against what?"

Again a pause of several heartbeats. *"Very well, human, since you insist upon hearing the naked truth: aside from the ever-present dangers represented by savages and the many voracious nonsentient life-forms dwelling within the Sea of Leaves, there happens to be you, yourself."*

Geanar's jaw dropped, but his expression of wounded innocence was lost over the radio. "Me? Of all people? Listen to me carefully, Hooded Seven, this is strictly a business proposition for me. Value for value, as the materialistic expression would have it: you're going to pay me for something you find more useful than money; I'm going to accept in exchange for something I value a great deal less than your money. Granted, the entire affair's crass and sordid and of no higher spiritual significance whatever, but what conceivable reason would I have to injure or

we will leave you to look to your own. Is this agreeable?"

Geanar grinned, this time fully aware his emotions were unknown to his listener. "Indeed it is, Hooded Seven, indeed it is. Both agreeable, I'd say, and inevitable."

"Far be it from us to disillusion you in that regard, human, but we feel obligated to point out that we—and our motivations—must surely be as alien and incomprehensible to you as you and yours are to us. But enough of this for now. Do whatever you think best about the presence of other parties at our meeting ground. When we speak again, it will be, as the saying goes, face-to-face."

"I shall," Geanar replied, feeling a sudden chill again and wondering why, "be looking forward to it."

suit, however, and given the level of technology the lamviin seemed to operate on, he was hesitant to ask Pemot for help.

While Middle C skinned and gutted his kill, a process much neater and quicker than the boy had ever imagined it could be, and started one of his miniscule and almost flameless camp fires, less easy than it looked as a scattering of raindrops began to fall all about them, the lamviin had resumed fiddling with his radio receiving gear again, taking elaborate care to keep it covered and dry.

"Well," he asserted, removing the earphones from his knee joint for a moment, "I believe we've now empirically established that neither the Antimacassarites nor the Securitasians are the source of those signals which I recorded earlier."

"Oh yeah?"

His other physical needs attended to, Mac had wandered nearer the lamviin, the sled, and the taflak's fire where the brace of spitted hare had begun sizzling, beginning to have some interest in food after all. Somewhere far away on the horizon an enormous and dazzling bolt of lightning leaped from the clouds, now a solid purple-black overhead, into the Sea of Leaves.

A loud crackle issued from Pemot's earphones, audible even where Mac stood. Mac counted a slow twenty-five before he heard a distant growl of thunder, and found himself hoping it had zapped CaptainMother b'Tehla right in her bustle.

"Good thing you weren't wearing those contraptions. How have we established that?"

Pemot attempted to wipe moisture from his carapace with a reflexive, almost uncontrollable shudder, much the same way a human being might react to finding a large, hairy spider crawling up the back of his neck. When it rained in the Fodduan capital city of Mathas, perhaps once every dozen Sodde Lydfan years—a fine, almost invisible mist adding up to a full hundredth of a lamviin finger's-width of precipitation—all traffic stopped, businesses and schools

ing a plastic-draped finger at the boy. "Pair-of-noia: an English pun, no better than the Fodduan variety."

"Shee no leek taflak?"

Mac shook his head to clear his ears. "Latin, actually—or maybe Greek. Maybe we could both switch to limericks, instead. And can't we do something constructive about Middle C's vowels, Pemot? Another few days of his dog-whistle accent, and I'll be stone deaf."

"What would you suggest?" asked Pemot. "Just talk, to him, to me. He'll eventually catch on."

He addressed the native. "No, my trusty warrior friend, Captain-Mother b'Tehla doesn't like taflak at all, and now, thanks to you and your spear thrower, she'll like them even less in future, I believe. She respects them, however, which was more than sufficient to our needs at that particular moment. Thank you, indeed, Middle C."

He repeated the native's real name.

Mac tried repeating it after him.

The native cringed and reeled off several paragraphs of high-frequency taflak chatter.

Pemot looked at Mac. "He asks whether he and I can't do something constructive to improve your accent."

The boy had never heard a lamviin giggle before.

Lightning struck again, this time much nearer by.

The lamviin's earphones crackled, thunder answering almost at once.

In a few seconds, rain began falling in a manner which even Mac would have agreed was a downpour.

Something *screamed.*

Before any of the three knew what had happened, the rainy night was filled with a different kind of roaring, as a hurricane seemed to begin to blow. Mac had a brief glimpse of a polished fiberplastic hull blurring by, leaped backward, and was missed by no more than inches when the hovercraft streaked past.

Inside the machine, a man-shaped figure raised a fist and shook it at them.

blindness—he squeezed the trigger, closing his eyes just beforehand.

Even through his tight-shut eyelids, he could see a ball of sunlike fury roar away into the night. It struck the hovercraft the slightest grazing blow and bounced into the foliage, burning its way down toward the surface of the planet.

As Mac opened his eyes, the first thing he saw was a yellow-white searchlight shaft, striking upward into the murky sky from where the plasma ball had begun tunneling. From somewhere within those violated depths, a horde of small, furry shapes poured up and outward, shoulder to shoulder, spreading across the sodden leaves and disappearing into them again. The hovercraft was spinning around and around like an insane top, still headed for them.

Pemot had begun firing now as well, holding his quaint reciprocating chemical-powered projectile pistol in all three hands, rested on one of the bundles in the sled.

Unnoticed, his protective tarpaulin had slipped off his rounded, shoulderless form.

Oblivious to the rain, which seemed to increase in volume every second he rocked back and forth, hands lifting with the recoil of each shot, keeping up a steady pulsing rhythm of gunfire—his weapon's muzzle flashes were short-lived globes of pale blue-pink in the inky darkness—until the magazine was empty. He ejected it with one hand, replaced it with the other, all the while keeping the gun trained on the vehicle with the third, and recommenced shooting.

Mac closed his eyes and fired again.

And again.

When he opened them, he saw the attacking machine had veered off at last. It still appeared to be out of control, spinning about its axis, but was slowing.

Off to one side, the shaft of plasma light winked out.

That, for the moment, at least, was the last he saw of the car, although he thought he heard it shudder

and English, he assured both of his offworld friends he was uninjured, thanks to an inborn reflex which had sent him burrowing into the leaves without a conscious thought, the moment he'd seen the danger coming.

Death, it seemed, had passed directly over him.

He, too, had been trying his best to kill the fusion-powered monster before it killed them.

He, too, had no idea whether they'd succeeded.

And what was worse, he'd brought them more bad news.

cacy and one of Pemot's personal favorites—boiled tea, and *kood* smoke.

At last, when the human and the Sodde Lydfan could stand the suspense no longer, Middle C took up his spear thrower and, with many a high-pitched warble and whistle, showed them both a feature of it which neither had known existed.

"He says," Pemot translated, "that, unlike Earthians and lamviin, who invented pockets because they seem to have convenient places on their anatomy to hang them—" The scientist patted the pockets covering the legs (or arms) of his own trousers (or tunic). It was more than just an illustrative gesture. He'd misplaced his monocle in the previous night's excitement and seemed lost without it. He'd already mourned the passing of his radio equipment which had been reduced to sodden junk. "The taflak, unblessed anatomically, have had to arrive at some alternative arrangement. He directs our attention to the handle end of his spear thrower."

This, it developed, was hollow, friction-sealed with a tapered plug. Thanks to his implant, Mac had followed more of the native's speech than perhaps Pemot suspected. Now he heard Middle C explain the courage and strength which obtaining the materials for a spear thrower required on this vegetation-covered planet.

"Branches large enough to make spear throwers—and spears themselves—come from deep beneath the Sea of Leaves, the deeper beneath the sea, the larger the branches. A warrior is required to burrow down and cut a branch of the correct shape and size. No one else may do it for him. It is one of the rites of adulthood."

"I'd wondered," Mac confessed. "There doesn't seem to be anything large enough on the surface."

Pemot blinked. "Yes. I gather it's also the source of the finer stems and branches their village platforms and dwellings are fashioned from, as well; although such materials as these must come from

Mac, would have indicated the spears if he hadn't spent them all on the hovercraft last night.

"You New Strangers are much the same," stated the native. *"You carry metal tokens for good people, and, for the decaying berries in your own bag, you carry death spewers."*

He laid a gentle tentacle first on the holstered reciprocating pistol attached to Pemot's upper leg, then on the Borchert & Graham plasma gun at Mac's side.

"I see what you're getting at, old fellow." Pemot blinked understanding. "But what—"

"It is not comfortable to tell you, although I must, that some entire tribes among the taflak have become decaying berries. Mostly tribes in the barren lands. They trade with the Old Strangers, exchanging their willingness to do evil for crazy coins." Now Middle C held up the roll of perforated candies.

Pemot answered, "Hmm."

"I get it," Mac offered. "New Strangers—us Confederates. Old Strangers are the First Wavers. Some tribes near the poles do their dirty work, for . . . candy?"

"Why," Pemot asked Middle C, "do you call them crazy coins?"

"Because, slipped around the end of one's tentacle, they dissolve slowly, and make you do crazy things."

Mac shook his head. "Candy's a drug for the taflak?"

"It would appear so," answered the lamviin. "And where, might I ask, did you acquire this?"

Middle C took the roll of candy and, rising, threw it as hard as he could out into the Sea of Leaves.

"After we fought the death machine, I scouted around. Polar tribes are coming this way, following the slave machines of the many wheeled tribe of Old Strangers. I sneaked into their encampment, listened to them talk, and took this to show you. They would travel much faster on their own, and we would be dead by now, except that they do their masters' bidding and come at their masters' pace."

"So," Mac translated, "the bad news is that more

"Not quite."

"Oh?"

"Yeah. I came here for the Brightsuit. I never intended to leave without it. And now, I may not be able to leave without it. Remember, it's essentially a one-man spaceship, complete with weaponry. If I can get it away from my—"

"Another if, MacBear. I never have more than three with my breakfast. I accept that we need to find your grandfather's hovercraft, for one reason or another. Therefore—"

"You want to go and look for the death machine?"

Mac laughed. "Yeah, as crazy as it seems, we do. Do you know where it is?"

"No, but I do not think it went far, and I should be able to find it easily. Should I do this now?"

"We'd appreciate it greatly—but do have a care, will you? You've none of your throwing spears left. Don't get too close until we're there to back you up."

"Agreed. I have acquired great respect for these death spewers you New Strangers carry. I will avoid any such that may be with the machine and await the protection of your own."

While Middle C departed to look for the damaged Trekmaster, Mac and Pemot cleaned up their camp, packed their remaining possessions, and stowed them on the sand-sled. Pemot even found his eyeglass, hanging by its ribbon from a broken radio antenna section. They hadn't been at it ten minutes, when they heard a loud hooting not far away. Looking up, they saw Middle C waving a pair of spears in the air, which he'd recovered from where they'd fallen the night before. He went on with his search as they continued with their camp chores.

The taflak hunter returned in half an hour with news. He'd found the Preble hovercraft upright and intact. Following his agreement with Pemot, he hadn't approached it, but he had a keen eye which had discerned no activity within it.

The pair of outworlders trudged off in the native's impatient wake.

lieve we should confer with our mutual taflak friend instead."

Middle C had been waiting, impatient, for the extra-Majestan council of war to conclude. Hearing Pemot's reference to him, he came closer and asked what was required of him.

"I hesitate," Pemot told him, "to send you into danger on our account, old fellow, but I should like to know if it's possible for you to burrow all the way to the hovercraft under the covering of leaves."

"I myself burrowed down over fifty body lengths to obtain this, my three-eyed friend, a mere half body length is playtime for children not yet hutbroken."

"Very well, we'll either await your signal to follow on the surface or your return to tell us it's unsafe."

"Why not follow him under the leaves?"

"What?"

"MacBear has a good idea. I burrow, you follow. It should not be more difficult than walking on the surface."

"Dear me, I—"

"Claustrophobic, Pemot?"

"Of course not! I'm simply cautious. Very well, for Triarch and Empire, and all that sort of dryrot, let us go forward!"

Middle C began to whirl, not tentacle-over-tentacle as he did when traveling on the surface, but about the axis of the tentacle he was using for a leg. In a twinkling, he sank into the leafy "ground" like a post-hole digger.

Before too many seconds had passed, the taflak had disappeared from sight, leaving a narrow, cylindrical tunnel behind him, perhaps four feet from side to side. For a moment, the noise of his passage—which sounded to Mac something like the ice crusher in Mr. Meep's kitchens—ceased, followed by several chirps and whistles.

"Hurry, my friends, before it can grow closed behind me!"

"He says," Pemot translated, "we must hurry, or—"

"Ghastly creature."

Pemot reholstered his reciprocator and drew a large, curved, gleaming knife.

The next rat which tried to bite the lamviin lost its head.

"In any event," Pemot went on, "for all we know, these leaves around us now may have begun their lives at the bottom of the sea, a full six miles below us, just last year."

Mac, who didn't have a large fighting knife and hadn't yet learned to reduce the power of his father's plasma gun—if it could be done—used the heavy barrel as a club to kill a rat the size of a small dog which had lunged for his ankle.

Squealing and whistling came from ahead of the lamviin. Middle C was disposing of rats by the tentacle-full, as if they were part of the worldwide hedge he bored through.

"I have never seen anything like this number of rats," whistled the native warrior, *"Something from below must have driven them up out of the leaves."*

Mac wiped blood and fur from the front sight of his pistol, looked at his hand, and shivered. "What do you think, Pemot? Could it have been the shooting last night, that one wild plasma ball of mine?"

"Or something else," observed the lamviin. "I don't believe that ball went deep enough."

"Turnover," the taflak commented as if he fought for his life every day in this manner, *"goes as deep as where the leaves begin, about thirteen hundred body lengths down. Further below, in the eternal darkness, something which is the essence of ugliness reigns in their place. Perhaps this is what we disturbed, and it disturbed the rats. Be quiet, now, my Stranger friends. It is not ever good to speak of such things, and here and now is a worse place and time than most."*

Mac looked down between his feet, imagining the black and horror-filled depths below them, and shuddered.

CHAPTER XXI:
Well-Chosen Words

Burrowing up through the covering of leaves while Middle C and Mac did their best to keep the rats from bothering him, Pemot raised an arm and thrust a sensitized smartsuit finger up over the bullet-riddled fuselage of the inert machine.

He yanked it back down.

"Here's where all our rats are coming from, gentlebeings."

The lamviin whispered, rolling his large eyes upward, toward the hovercraft, as he did so. "They're flattened against the windows. The thing's jammed to the scuppers with them!"

In the comical squeak which served his species as a whisper, Middle C wanted to know how Pemot could say that without—apparently—looking. Also, what scuppers were.

Keeping his own voice low, Mac explained the various optical capabilities of smartsuits, which could be programmed to look like weather-beaten jeans or any other kind of clothing. The more accomplished and expensive models could also receive light on any portion of their surfaces and retransmit it to the inside of the hood, which Pemot had pulled up over his eyes before surveying the car.

Mac also confessed he didn't know what scuppers were, annoyed that an alien should have a better

boy had to be watchful to keep both thumbs—by Middle C, the lamviin, and the taflak's pair of long-bladed spears.

In a few moments, the mesh had been opened, and they were standing on top of the machine.

"All together now!" Pemot's voice was no longer soft. "One, two, *three!*"

He and Mac and Middle C began jumping up and down on the battle-scorched body of the car, screaming as loud as they could and banging on it with whatever implements they had. The hovercraft bounced on its resilient skirt, sinking a trifle deeper into the leaves. A dark, furry, squeaking torrent issued from the broken windows, vibrating the machine as the thousands—or, as it seemed to Mac, millions—of rats it was composed of jostled one another where the frame constricted the flow, and leaving a thick, rich, nauseating smell in its wake.

Mac's eyes watered. He coughed and went on jumping, landing hard on both heels, firing his plasma gun into the air, burst upon burst. Even in full daylight the five megawatt flash was dazzling, and he felt deafened by its sharp-edged roar.

Pemot's eyes watered. He sneezed through all six nostrils and continued jumping, as well—six feet to Mac's two—banging on the already dented roof as he did so with the butt end of the spear he'd borrowed from Middle C.

Middle C's eye turned a slight yellow, but, although he only had one leg to jump with, he followed Pemot's example, relying on his other spear and the end of his spear thrower to contribute to the terrifying racket they were trying to make.

They went on with the performance until they were all three hoarse and exhausted, the hovercraft had sunk to its scuppers—whatever they might be—in the Sea of Leaves, and what they hoped was the last rat had squeaked with indignation at its tormentors, lashed its pink and naked tail, and abandoned the damaged car.

Mac sat down on the roof of the Trekmaster, el-

of the thousands of rodents which they'd driven away. The floor carpet had been eaten down to perforated chrome-magnesium and fiberglass. The wall fabric and headliner had vanished. Even the four seats were no more than skeletons of steel.

And on one of them sat a skeleton of bone.

"MacBear . . ." Pemot's voice was as gentle as he could make it. "Was this your grandfather?"

Mac looked across the seat backs at the skeleton.

It was clean and polished. Here and there a toothmark showed where the rats had been trying to get to the marrow. No doubt they'd been interrupted by the noise on the roof. Still held together by their drying tendons, the bones looked like a schoolroom demonstration model. Nothing whatever remained to identify them.

"I don't know." The boy's answer wavered, his stomach feeling uncertain. "I—hold on, what's this?"

He leaned forward and picked up the tattered spine of a hard-backed book. Nothing was left of the pages, but the rats hadn't cared for the plastic cover.

"*The Confessions of Frater Jimmy-Earl.* It's my grandfather, all right—Dalmeon Geanar."

Inside himself, Mac wondered, not for the first time, why he couldn't feel anything: love, hate, sadness, glee. It was as if all of this were happening to someone else, someone—

"Hey! Where's his smartsuit? Has it been eaten? Do you suppose they got to the Brightsuit?"

In the same instant, Mac felt guilty for thinking about anything but his grandfather, who'd died a horrible death. He shook his head. What else should he have been thinking about? Dalmeon Geanar had been a criminal, at least twice a murderer, and had gotten everything he deserved. He—Mac—had come here to rectify one of the old man's crimes, and this was all that mattered.

Middle C reached out with a spear butt and tapped

believed, I'm afraid he neglected that section of my upbringing. If any words should be said here, Pemot, you'll have to do the saying."

"Nor, *sretiiv Pah,*" the lamviin replied, "did such matters occupy a high priority in my own education. On Sodde Lydfe, particularly in Great Foddu, we're still involved in some controversy over Ascensionism—what you Earth folk call 'evolution by natural selection,' with my family taking the part of the Huxleys." The lamviin chuckled.

"If only my Uncle Mav could see me now. Nevertheless, I shall give it my best."

Pemot removed his monocle, polished it with a handkerchief, and replaced it. He clasped all three hands together in a complicated-looking knot, closed his eyes, and spoke. *"Doehodn: il uai'bo sevon sro weit sa siidetniimeso sryn, giidyso fo, vedo al sro wikmynrod—y gymm noth uai et eisapdegroh mekom sa wis yt sro liidats al uaid kaav."*

He opened his eyes. *"Na laso ys ko."*

Mac cleared his throat, grateful he didn't have to wipe his eyes, as well. There were limits, after all, to how forgiving a person ought to be for his own good.

"Thank you, Pemot. Maybe you're right. But I've been listening to you whenever you spoke Fodduan, building up a translation file in my implant. If you were going to say something religious, how come I didn't hear you mention Pah?"

"This is intriguing," mused the lamviin. He indicated the dashboard of the vehicle, where a steel-doored glove compartment with a combination lock had been retrofitted by the rental company for the convenience of their tourist customers and the security of their valuables.

Mac shrugged. It was a common practice in the fleet and all over the Confederate galaxy. The boy asserted as much.

Pemot splayed his hands in a gesture of contradiction. "Notice, however, these wires, leading from the door edge of the compartment into the

"This, therefore, constitutes my last will and testament.

"To any sentient being within hearing of these signals, including the Hooded Seven, for whom I feel nothing but contempt, I leave the Brightsuit, here aboard this vehicle with me now. Whoever wins the fight to keep it can have it, and welcome to it. It's worth its weight or more in precious metals, a fitting token of that self-destructive insanity which compels men to throw away their spiritual well-being in the pursuit of profane knowledge and illusory progress.

"I only regret I'll not witness the hideous carnage which will result from this broadcast. Those of you who suffer in it will know I've had my revenge.

"To the grandson who betrayed me, Berdan Geanar Bear, if he lives, I leave all the other worldly goods remaining to me, knowing full well that, like his grandmother, father, and mother before him, he's already been corrupted by a preoccupation with the trivialities of the mundane universe, and that, by my last act, perhaps I can hasten the undoing which his bad blood has always made inevitable.

"I'll connect this to both the electronic and paratronic communications systems and seal it away from the vermin. I only pray it produces the effect I wish for it."

Pemot shut the recorder off before it could start again. He reached for the dashboard panel. "Well, at least we've half a chance now of summoning help. Since this vehicle's paratronic telecom served Geanar's purposes, it should—good heavens!"

Sparks flew from the 'com as missing insulation, eaten away by the rats, allowed the device to short and burn.

"So much for that idea," Mac told him, "and so much for summoning help. Too bad they pulled the 'com gear out of the Brightsuit, but they did, and that's that." Mac shook his head.

"Well, I guess there's no need to ask where all our trouble's coming from anymore. Surely the

dle C. Let's attend to getting the crate open. Perhaps our salvation lies with its contents. If not, then perhaps, damaged as it is, we should attempt to repair this much-abused machine."

Ivanhoe, and King Arthur, frowned at the verbal in-
trusion. The thing before him was too lovely for
words.

Even Middle C was speechless, leaning closer on
his single leg, humming wordlessly and tunelessly
as he examined his own curve-distorted reflection.

Some remnant of the Brightsuit's titanic energy
must have augmented what they all saw. No mirror
had ever been made which could produce a clearer,
more flawless image. It was as if the finish on the
surface was spring water, fathoms deep. Whatever
else the three companions noticed, it occurred to each
of them that, despite all of its rough handling, its
many years of storage and neglect, the Brightsuit
didn't show the slightest sign of wear or of accumu-
lated grime: not a dent, not a scratch, not so much
as a dust speck or a fingerprint.

At last, Mac had to touch it. To his surprise, it was
as flexible as any smartsuit, perhaps even more so.
Beneath his fingers, which left no print behind when
he lifted them, it felt like sheer silk covering warm
human flesh.

The wreckage of the hovercraft rocked with the
force of a nearby explosion.

Another explosion thundered, even closer this
time. The noise was excruciating.

Leaving the Brightsuit, Mac and his companions
rushed to the open gull-wing door. From the north-
east, they saw the Antimacassarite vehicle A.L.N.
Compassionate bearing down upon them, its twin
screws turning as fast as the slaves could be driven
around the threads. As they ran, flames spurted from
the weapons along the flying forecastle, threatening
to roast anyone who got in the vehicle's path.

What was worse, tumbling cylindrical projectiles
were rising in high-topped arcs from launchers on
the quarterdeck, falling to one side or the other of
the *Compassionate*, and burying themselves deep in
the moss where they exploded, showering vegetation
and metal fragments back up in a wide-mouthed,
deadly funnel.

Meanwhile, Mac had found the seams. "You can say that again—hey! Pemot, it's shrinking around my legs! It's making itself fit!"

The lamviin gave his equivalent of a shrug. "I don't suppose they call them smartsuits for nothing. Here, get your left arm in here, and consider yourself lucky not to have nine limbs to deal with, squeezing into this suit. Getting dressed always seems to take me forever."

Mac smoothed the front seam in place. He took the flexible hood in his hands, where, like all smartsuit hoods in proper repair, it lay hanging across his chest.

"Well, Pemot, here goes!" He lifted the hood over his face, sealed it at the back of his head, and took an experimental breath. The air collected and processed by the surface of the suit was clean, cool, and dry. The inside surface of the garment began cleansing the boy's skin, treating minor cuts, bruises, and abrasions he'd been accumulating, killing microorganisms, adjusting his metabolism to conditions in which the human race hadn't evolved and couldn't adjust to by themselves. It was the first time he'd been comfortable since coming to Majesty.

"But I still can't—oh yes I can! Pemot, all I had to do was think about being able to see, and suddenly I could!"

"Certainly," the lamviin replied, "your cerebrocortical implant detected the desire and transmitted it to the Brightsuit as a command. Your old suit must have been in terrible condition, MacBear, as this feature is nothing at all revolutionary, any more than is the fact we can hear one another perfectly, although separated by near-perfect insulation. However, I'd be careful, young friend, with this new suit. Considering its alleged capabilities, such a response to your wish could be a dangerous thing, indeed."

"I will be, Pemot."

He stood up, an eerie, mirror-surfaced mannikin, an animated chromium statue. If anything, the

them had guessed. He could see several other vehicles coming now, characteristic of both nation-states.

Uncoordinated as they may have been, they formed a solid ring of death around Dalmeon Geanar's ruined hovercraft and the offworld travelers who'd discovered it. But something else was happening as well, something vaster and more ominous. Inside the deadly circle formed by the enemy vehicles, not a thousand yards from the spot where Pemot stood, the Sea of Leaves appeared to be boiling.

The moss churned and rippled with the force of something coming up from beneath it.

Something enormous and powerful.

It was at this point Mac noticed he'd left his Borchert & Graham behind in the hovercraft.

He was distracted by a puff of smoke from aboard the A.L.N. *Compassionate.* Polished, helpless-looking target in the sky that he appeared, he'd begun to draw enemy gunfire. Without his prompting, a hair-fine beam of brilliance, blinding even through his hood, leaped out from the Brightsuit near the back of his hand. Another puff blossomed in mid-air as it vaporized the rising bullet.

This first shot was followed by a ragged and spontaneous volley. Each bullet was converted to plasma hundreds of feet away from its intended destination. Mac watched with amplified vision as Leftenant Commander MacRame shouted at the rifle squad, lined them up, and commanded them to make their fire simultaneous.

A dozen beams flashed out to counteract the Leftenant Commander's military discipline.

Mac was just as surprised when—perhaps because he'd thought of how exposed and conspicuous he was, perhaps because the Brightsuit was reaching the limit of its bullet-destroying capacities—he was whisked upward several hundred yards. At the same time, the surface of the Brightsuit was transformed from perfect reflectivity, to a perfect match for the pure blue of the sky.

pole, was Talisman. Both were invisible, far below the horizon at this altitude.

A peculiar surge of pressure ran up his spine.

He realized the Brightsuit had "overheard" his thoughts and begun rising again to some altitude from which he might see the poles. He stopped it where the sky was even blacker than before. The stars seemed like hard, cold chips of diamond.

What should he do now? Where should he go? All he knew for certain was that his friends, Pemot and Middle C, needed help, and none was to be found within thousands of miles.

He'd help them himself.

Firming his will, he ordered the Brightsuit to take him down. As friction with the thickening air heated the outside surface of the suit, it began to throw off excess energy in the form of radiation in the visible spectrum.

Inside, the temperature remained constant.

At last, glowing much too bright to be looked at, he swooped like a bird of prey to meet the foe.

The first to feel his wrath was the *Compassionate,* just a few yards from collision with the ruined Trek-master—where Pemot stood, pistol braced and ready, just inside the door—and already spewing uniformed and moss-shoed rifle bearers. A brilliant beam from each wrist of the Brightsuit traced fiery lines along the *Compassionate*'s bow and quarterdeck, splitting the vessel into ponderous, reeling halves which wandered away from one another, spilling slaves who tumbled off into the leaves.

With another gesture Mac drew a line of flame between the hovercraft and the advancing troops. One or two foolish enough to surge onward, despite his warning, exploded like popcorn kernels at the touch of a blinding wire-fine beam.

The rest halted and threw down their weapons, which sank into the sea like stones in pond water.

A Securitasian crankapillar three times the size of the *Intimidator* launched a pair of fireballs straight at the helpless hovercraft. Fire met fire as Mac's en-

When it had gone, nothing but a shallow, smoldering, conical depression remained.

And even this had soon begun to fill in, softened and eradicated by the restless Sea of Leaves.

had discovered they liked being free—and uneaten. Others, like Leftenant Commander Goldberry MacRame, with her hair hanging down in limp strings and her sopping uniform already beginning to shrink, hadn't been amused at all.

"I say," the lamviin told his friend, "it would appear we've a substantial greeting party."

Pemot was right. Waiting at the bottom of the long ladder was a small crowd of well-wishers, all of them waving and yelling at the tops of their voices. The first individual Mac recognized, from his tall, battered plug hat and the eternal dark aroma of his pipe, already wafting up the staircase, was A. Hamilton Spoonbender.

Impatient, the man bounded up the stairs to seize Mac's hand. "You did it, Berdan, my boy! Blast me, I never really believed you would, but you did it!"

Mac was forced to clamp his teeth together to keep from chipping them and biting his tongue until the museum owner was through jerking his arm back and forth. Feeling shy, he grinned, discovering he didn't know what to say. "I, uh . . ."

"Let's get down on terra firma—and believe me, the more firma, the less terra—the whole gang's here to see you, boy, custom delivered by a chauffeured private starship. Everybody, including—"

"Who's your handsome sidekick, Berdan?"

This from the female lamviin, Miss Nredmoto *Ommot* Uaitiip who, as the three reached ground level at long last, seemed to be looking Pemot over with more than casual interest.

"I, madame," replied the scientist, "am Epots Dinnomm *Pemot*, at your service and pleased to meet you. Our mutual friend now travels under the name MacDougall Bear."

"Likewise, I'm sure. Whatever he's calling himself, a lot of high-powered talent's waiting to see him."

Mac blinked, but it wasn't the equivalant of a nod. "What do you mean, Ommot?"

Spoonbender turned to Bertram and grinned a toothy grin. He turned back to the boy. "Don't let me down. Be sure you hold them up piratically, Ber—Mac, for they're well and truly desperate, I assure you, and can certainly afford it."

Bertram looked exasperated. "Thanks a lot, Spoonbender." The businessman shrugged and grinned. "But what the dirty dishes. You brought it back to us, didn't you, Mac—or should I say Mr. Bear? I knew your dad and mom. Let me tell you, they'd be proud of you today. Why, that's his Borchert & Graham you're wearing, isn't it?"

Mac didn't hear the question, he was busy feeling what he was supposed to, when he was supposed to, and wiping tears out of his eyes as a consequence.

"I don't understand this," he answered at last. "You and your—Professor Thorens—you don't owe me anything. It's still your suit. My grandfa—Dalmeon Geanar stole it to sell to the Hooded Seven, whoever they are, and I got it back for you because of my folks. And because I was ashamed."

With enormous effort, he stifled a sob. Instead, he turned his back to regain control of himself, and, without warning, felt a soft, warm hand on the back of his neck.

"What are you doing to this boy, Freeman?" The voice was soft and warm, as well.

"Dora Jayne, my dear, this is no mere boy you're fondling, but a man in every sense of the word, just returned triumphant from the savage jungle! And by the way, since you're a married woman, I'll thank you to stop fondling him."

"Oh, Freeman, you're so cute when you're jealous!"

Mac turned and gazed into the bottomless azure eyes of the galaxy's most famous—and most beautiful—physicist.

The business arrangements with Laporte Paratronics were simple and straightforward. Mac had recovered the suit, for which Bertram and Thorens felt he was owed a fee. In addition, because the suit

ward, to treat his injuries or save himself from the rats."

Pemot's fur indicated a shrug, followed by a shiver. It had been too cold for his peace of mind, even on the equator.

"I hesitate to point out that the man was your grandfather, MacBear, and that, if you can't answer a question like that, I certainly can't be expected to."

Mac laughed. "You're a big help. Okay, let me see: he knew the suit worked. It wasn't the dangerous failure he made everybody think it was. But what was it to him? A valuable commodity, something to be stolen and sold, like a bag of money, or a—"

"Or a fur coat," Pemot suggested. "I doubt whether many mink thieves try on every coat they steal."

"Vehicle thieves surely do," argued Mac. "People who steal hovercraft or spaceships have to drive away what they've stolen. But to grandfa—Geanar, I mean, the Brightsuit wasn't the vehicle it is in fact, but a suit of clothes."

Pemot blinked. "And so, he adopted the fur thief's attitude, rather than the hovercraft thief's?"

"Yeah, I guess that's the closest we'll ever get to understanding what happened—unless we just say he was a self-made loser and leave it at that."

The lamviin blinked again. "Well I'm glad you were the one to say it, MacBear. I should have been reluctant to do so."

Mac grinned, reached down a hand, and patted the distinguished xenopraxeologist on his furry cara-pace. It was a stroke of fortune that Pemot had been fully suited up when Mac had grabbed him off the Trekmaster. They'd later learned that close proxim-ity to the Brightsuit in full-powered flight could cause severe tachyon burns.

"I can understand that."

"And," Pemot observed, "I suppose we'll leave the mystery of the Hooded Seven for another time. It

BIO OF A SPACE TYRANT
Piers Anthony

"Brilliant...a thoroughly original thinker and storyteller with a unique ability to posit really *alien* alien life, humanize it, and make it come out alive on the page." *The Los Angeles Times*

A COLOSSAL NEW FIVE VOLUME SPACE THRILLER—
BIO OF A SPACE TYRANT
The Epic Adventures and Galactic Conquests of Hope Hubris

VOLUME I: REFUGEE   84194-0/$3.50 US/$4.50 Can
Hubris and his family embark upon an ill-fated voyage through space, searching for sanctuary, after pirates blast them from their home on Callisto.

VOLUME II: MERCENARY   87221-8/$3.50 US/$4.50 Can
Hubris joins the Navy of Jupiter and commands a squadron loyal to the death and sworn to war against the pirate warlords of the Jupiter Ecliptic.

VOLUME III: POLITICIAN   89685-0/$3.50 US/$4.50 Can
Fueled by his own fury, Hubris rose to triumph obliterating his enemies and blazing a path of glory across the face of Jupiter. Military legend...people's champion...promising political candidate...he now awoke to find himself the prisoner of a nightmare that knew no past.

THE BEST-SELLING EPIC CONTINUES—
VOLUME IV: EXECUTIVE
89834-9/$3.50 US/$4.50 Can
Destined to become the most hated and feared man of an era, Hope would assume an alternate identify to fulfill his dreams ...and plunge headlong into madness.

VOLUME V: STATESMAN
89835-7/$3.50 US/$4.95 Can
the climactic conclusion of Hubris' epic adventures:

AVON Paperbacks